THE ALIEN'S FALCONER

USA TODAY BESTSELLING AUTHORS

ARIZONA TAPE
SKYE MACKINNON

http://www.skyemackinnon.com
http://arizonatape.com

Cover by Peryton Covers.
Illustration by Adrian DKC.
Formatting by Peryton Press.

CONTENTS

[1]

GEORGIA

I carefully manoeuvred through the thick jungle part of the planet, the rough orange leaves threatening to cut the underside of my arms. Luckily, I was wearing my makeshift guards. That was the advantage of camping somewhere familiar.

And Planet Bevba was definitely familiar. To most, it was just one of the many deserted island planets around the Tarran sun, but it was my playground..

A shrill cry alerted me to the menace from above, and I held up my hand to receive the visitor. A medium-sized bird with blue wings attempted to land on my forearm, his sharp talons scratching into the material of my brace as he missed his landing. He crashed into the sharp plants in front of me, and it wasn't the first time I was glad he was covered in scales to protect him.

"You're no falcon, are you?" I said, sighing as I plucked him from the mess.

Aba let out a soft thrilling noise. "No falcon," he mimicked.

A pang of longing shot through me as it always did whenever he repeated something I said. As human as it sounded, it was nothing compared to the real thing. A real conversation with someone who cared.

This was as close as it got.

I plucked some of the thorns from his scaly chest and he looked at me with adoration in his four eyes.

"Four eyes and still no depth of vision, huh?" I teased while stroking the top of his head where his feathers were the softest. As much as I liked ribbing on him, he was my dearest companion and I wouldn't trade him for anything. Not for all the money in the world or the fattest cargo ship in the galaxy. Maybe for a Mister Whippy from the seaside, *maybe,* but only if he was particularly annoying that day.

My mouth salivated just from thinking about ice cream and I quickly pushed the thoughts to the back of my mind. There was no use longing for something I couldn't get.

Aba whistled to himself as I let him ride on my arm and I enjoyed the familiar weight. It reminded me of when I trained birds of prey with my grandfather and it was moments like this that made me feel like myself.

I trekked through the wilderness until I arrived at the landing site of my space shuttle and Aba flew up, cawing happily at the sight of home. The loading bay door slid open when it sensed the unlocking technology embedded in my shoulder, a crude piece of technology compared to what was out there, but it did the job.

I instantly felt a sense of relief as I got out of the sun. Even though these planets circled around a yellow star, it was much harsher than what I was used to, certainly compared to the poor excuse of summer in England.

"I need some more sunblock," I told Aba.

"Sunblock. I need more sunblock," he replied, flying up from my arm. "Sunblock! That damned sun is going to kill me one day!"

There was something uncanny about hearing my own words echoed back to me, especially things I said a while ago. It made me hopeful that one day, he could master the language and say things of his own though. One day, maybe.

I unlocked the second door to the main part of the ship by pressing my hand on the modified scanner.

"Welcome back, Captain Georgia," an automated voice said.

"Good to be back," I replied gruffly.

The doors slid open while simultaneously locking the loading bay behind me. If there was anything I'd learned from my time in space, it was to never leave anything unlocked. That was a cardinal rule.

I did a quick check around as I walked in but everything was how I left it. Perks of being on an uninhabited piece of land. Besides, what could people want from this piece of junk?

Aba flew towards the pile of pillows that was his bed, landing badly in it. He was definitely not made for confined living spaces but it wasn't like I kept him on a string. He was free to go if he wished.

I pulled my arm guards off and put them back in their compartment by the door. They were starting to get worn out but I didn't have the material to fix them up.

"Shall we listen to some music?" I proposed, hitting the old radio I acquired not that long ago. It sprung to life and an unfamiliar song came on through the static. It sounded Ralish or maybe even Kyvenish in genre, not that I cared. None of those were planets worth visiting. The aliens there were just like anywhere else, cold, foreign, and without compassion for someone like me. To them, I was just a non-Galactic entity without rights, something that had been made clear to me time and time again.

I involuntarily traced the raised scars on my underarms, memories of a time I'd rather forget.

"Maybe no music," I decided. I turned the radio off and made it through the living space into the small kitchenette. My stomach rumbled and I searched the cupboards for something easy to eat but came up short. My last haul hadn't been very successful and it showed in the sad selection of canned food I had left.

I selected a packet of ship crackers and some pink slurry in a jar that didn't taste unlike mashed potatoes when heated right. It would do for my immediate hunger, but it wasn't exactly a good home-cooked meal. For that, I'd have to go 'foraging' first.

Aba watched me with four greedy eyes when I sat on the threadbare sofa and started munching my food.

"You had an entire snake yesterday, you don't need any food for at least a week," I told him sternly. That bird was prone to overeating, which usually resulted in me having to clean the ship. Even at three years old, he still hadn't learned that he only needed to eat every ten days or so. Or maybe he simply didn't want to understand.

I reached for my tablet, cringing at the cracks on the screen. I really needed a new one soon, but none of the ships I'd encountered recently had contained tech compatible with my own ancient vessel. One day, I'd have to upgrade, but my entire process depended on having an old ship. The ruse wouldn't be as believable with a modern starcruiser, as much as I'd prefer to live in one.

Repressing a sigh, I swiped through the maps of the sector, plotting my route. As nice as it had been to feel solid ground beneath my feet, I never stayed in any place for long. Even though I hated to admit it, the B3RR-Y had become my home. Not that I'd ever admit that to anyone, not even Aba. The alien parrot was still eyeing me jealously. At least he didn't beg for food. Despite his intelligence, it wasn't easy to train him, mostly because he was a moody male who refused to do my bidding ninety per cent of the time. The fact that he was behaving now probably meant that he had plans to make my life difficult later on. As much as I loved the silly bird, he was also a pain in the arse.

I was so lost in thought that I hadn't realised I'd eaten the last spoonful of pink slurry. I was still hungry. Ugh. I didn't feel like foraging. It was time to leave this planet and go back to work.

"Ready for takeoff," I announced, waiting for my avian echo. Aba promptly repeated my words. If he'd been human, I would have interpreted his chirpy voice as joy, but it was hard to tell for sure. I sometimes suspected that I read too much into Aba's behaviour, seeing emotions and intention where there was only mimicry. I knew nothing about his species. Stars, I didn't even know if he really was a male. If I had friends, I'd ask them what he was exactly. No, first I'd tell them the story of how I'd almost eaten him as an egg. That would make them laugh. We'd laugh together, slap each others' backs, then someone else would tell an equally funny story.

"Ready for takeoff," Aba cawed for a second time as if to remind me that I had work to do.

"Thanks, buddy. You're right, dwelling on the impossible isn't good for me. Let's get off this planet. Time to fly."

Aba shook his wings in agreement and flew over to the main console, landing in his favourite spot where he had the perfect view of both me in my chair and the large, if slightly blurry, viewscreen.

I entered our course and crossed my fingers. With a bit of luck, I'd eat a proper meal soon.

[2]

ELLABEE

Some days, I hated being in charge. Every time I thought I'd have a moment to myself, someone else came to ask for my permission, advice or simply seemed to seek my company. I glared at Katak's back as he shuffled off, clearly not happy with the answer I'd given the pilot. It wasn't my fault that he'd had to move into a smaller cabin. Space on the PoTA-2 was limited and now that we had another mated couple on board, I'd had to make changes. I'd given Katak an extra day off to make up for it, but he still wasn't satisfied. So be it. As much as I wanted my crew to be happy, I also valued my reputation as a strict captain. I had to set boundaries and rules.

I cautiously looked around the bridge. Everyone was focused on their consoles, ignoring me. Finally, this was the moment I'd been waiting for.

"Crew, I'll be in my quarters," I announced. I'd be relaxing in my soft podchair in just a few clicks. "If you need any-"

With a soul-destroying beep, the emergency sensor flickered to life.

Rak. Seriously? This was the worst timing ever.

I forced down the string of curses threatening to spill from my lips and turned to Lini. "What's triggered the alarm?"

"A nearby vessel is sending an emergency signal. I'm having trouble receiving more than just a basic life sign from the ship."

"Show me the ship on the screen. Inil, scan on all frequencies. I want to know what's going on."

The small green Biblib nodded which made his mohawk bounce. "Aye, Captain."

I turned towards the left cockpit where my pilot was being distracted by her mate. I couldn't be too mad since Atina had been a lot happier since Heather joined our crew, but still, this was not the time for frolicking.

To break them up, I snapped my fingers at them. "This is not the time."

The two broke apart, both with a sheepish look on their face. Even if Atina was the normal Kyven blue and Heather had pale skin from her Earth planet, it was true what they said about couples who spent too much time together. They did start to look alike.

"Sorry, Captain," Atina said, turning her attention to the command.

Heather chuckled awkwardly. "Yes, sorry. I'll get out of your hair."

I involuntarily touched my braids, confused about what she meant until I remembered that they used a lot of weird expressions on their Earth Planet. I could ask for clarification but this was not the time. She was leaving, that was all I wanted.

"Lini, what did the scan reveal?" I called, keeping a close eye on the map.

"Distress signal has come from an Xcruiser174. That's a small vessel, four-unit capacity. The signal was sent 24 clicks ago and I located it to Planet Torrap." Lini said as he ran a hand through his colourful mohawk. "I also did another scan, we're the only ship within a xx radius."

That was bothersome. Planet Torrap was only a small detour but that wasn't my main issue with the situation. Depending on what we'd find, it would delay our course and shipments which was an issue by itself. Delayed shipments meant dissatisfied clients and dissatisfied clients meant no payment.

But on the other hand, could I really ignore a distress signal?

"Lini, is your brother healthy enough to function?

"Inil is virus-free, Captain."

"Good. I want a report of our ship. Are we in any condition to respond to this emergency call?"

The eyes on the back of Lini's head opened and turned red as he performed a diagnostic scan. It was good to have them back in shape and able to run the ship.

Lini turned around to give his twin on the other side of his head a chance to talk in his monotone voice. "System scan complete. PoTA-2 is operating at optimum capacity. Energy reserves, five out of seven. Food reserves, nine out of eleven. Weight capacity, four out of five. We are ahead of schedule by twelve centi-clicks."

Those were good numbers. It certainly confirmed that we could make a detour and help the Xcruiser174, even if it was at full capacity.

"Atina, set course towards the vessel. Approach with caution. We don't know what condition the ship is in. Let's stay clear of any explosions this time," I said.

They all sprung into action, not needing any further instruction from me. Despite my exhaustion, I couldn't help but feel proud of my crew. Receiving an SOS from a ship in peril didn't happen very often. I couldn't even remember the last time we'd responded to an emergency like this. Space was so vast that we rarely ever encountered another vessel outside the main shipping routes. Right now, we were quite a distance from the closest space station, with just a few uninhabited planets showing up on the star map. What were the chances of us being here just at the right time to come and help the stricken ship?

The signal grew stronger as we neared the planet. Another scan brought up a more accurate picture of what we were getting into and I could make out the

Xcruiser174 stranded on a flat meadow with yellow grass. The image was blurry but I could make out some dark smoke and what looked like perhaps a dent in one of the wings. I wasn't an expert in these kinds of vessels but it looked like an unfortunate crash.

They were lucky we'd received their distress signal.

"Do we know how many sentient life forms we're dealing with yet?" I asked.

Lini activated another scanner. "Looks like just one, but I can't get a data code. It's saying Unknown, so it must be a sentient entity that isn't part of the Galactic Union. Shall we return?"

That made the situation a little trickier. The guidebook of the Galactic Union strongly advised limiting contact with non-Galactic Union beings, but there was another code that I abided by that overruled any suggestions from the GU. The code of a Kyven Captain.

"Keep going down and send a reply to their distress signal," I said firmly. I didn't know exactly what we were going to find on landing and maybe it wasn't the smartest to stray from our route, but I wasn't going to turn down a call for help.

[3]

GEORGIA

A large ship temporarily blocked the harsh sun as it descended from the sky and I jumped up, waving my arms to get their attention. A universal distress signal that seemed to work no matter where I was in space. I'd chosen Tarrop, a small planet with breathable air, as the place for my supposed crash. Behind me, smoke was rising from the B3RR-Y and I'd spread some random ship parts all over the sandy ground to make it look more real.

Aba cawed and rose from the seat next to me. I caught him before he could fly away.

"Stay here, you silly bird, or it'll turn you into minced meat," I chided him.

"Minced meat," he echoed cheerily.

I shielded my eyes as I looked up. The ship coming

down looked medium-sized and modified to carry cargo which was fantastic. That was just what I needed to restock my own supplies.

A small voice in the back of my head chided me for using this distress ruse to trick people but I squashed it quickly. It was dangerous to feel compassion and empathy for aliens, a lesson I'd learned a long time ago. Besides, it wasn't like I was harming anyone. If my rescuers were kind, I never took more than I needed. If they weren't kind... then they deserved this.

The ship's boosters came on as it landed on the other side of the meadow, just like they always did. It was a natural landing strip that no pilot could resist. That put them right where I wanted them.

"Go on, then," I told Aba, letting him go so he could investigate. I knew he'd be back in time for the fun to start; he always was.

He flew towards the ship, and I resisted the urge to follow him. It was always better if I let them come to me. Safer. If they were unsavoury, it wouldn't be hard to get my ship up and running and get the hell out of here.

After a small wait, two figures emerged from their loading dock. Even from a distance, it was easy to identify them as aliens from Kyven. They were humanoid in many ways except for their deep blue skin, their sixth finger, and surely some other features that I hadn't discovered yet and had no desire to either. While they looked human, they definitely weren't.

When they were more than halfway, I got up from

the log I was using as a seat so I could go towards them. Now that they were closer, I could make out that they were both female.

I held up my hand and clicked a simple greeting in their native language. "Hello."

The Kyven on the right, a woman with night-blue skin and silver-white hair in braids that I was instantly jealous of, nodded in acknowledgement. "Hello. Did you send out a distress signal?"

"Yes. I land bad. I crash here, I need help," I replied, my tongue already hurting from a simple sentence. It wasn't a language that came natural to me but I could understand it fairly well, which put me at an advantage.

The other female eyed me curiously. "Where did you learn to speak our language?"

I was starting to regret using the meet-and-greet ruse instead of ambushing them. It was going to take time. Still, this one usually ended without bloodshed.

"I had... crew colleague. Kyven. He teach me."

Such a euphemism. Klen had tortured me for his amusement. He'd left me with a rudimentary understanding of his native language, along with scars and nightmares. These were the first Kyvens I'd met since my escape. A cold shudder ran down my back despite the glaring sun above us. Not a memory I wanted to dwell on.

"Engine wrong," I continued, gesturing to my ship. "Can you help?"

"I'm Captain Ellabee," the braided woman

introduced herself. "I'm not an expert in mechanics, but Ja'lal here will take a look at your engine. If you don't need any medical assistance, I shall return to my ship and will await Ja'lal's report."

No, I needed both of them to go inside.

"Aba hurt."

I hated having to use my pet as an excuse, but the little bugger would probably love to be involved in this deception. His naughty streak had got him in trouble more than once.

"Who is Aba?" Captain Ellabee asked with a frown. Interesting, I didn't know Kyvens frowned like humans.

"My... don't know word. Come in."

I wasn't sure if she believed my excuse, but when I stepped back into the ship, both women followed me. Nice. Step one was completed. Time for step two.

While walking further into the B3RR-Y, I discreetly started a subroutine programmed into the ship's AI. I hadn't written the code myself, my tech skills were way too rudimentary for that, but you could get anything and everything on the black market. It had been one of my best purchases ever.

I mentally counted down from five, making sure I was past the barely visible mark on the wall, and waited for the siren.

It was so shrill I wanted to cover my ears, but for the ruse to be effective, I had to look as surprised as my two visitors. I turned to them, faking a look of shock, before the heavy fire locks slammed shut between us, sealing them in. I double checked that the locks behind them had also closed before hurrying to the bridge.

"Fire, fire!" Aba welcomed me happily, perching on the back of my chair.

"Yes, clever bird. And what comes next?"

"Next. Next. Next."

"No, that wasn't the right answer." I patted the sleek scales on his head. They instantly turned from pale gold to a shimmering ruby red. The colour change had only started once he'd reached maturity - or at least that's what I thought had happened when he'd stopped growing. Now, his scales reminded me of one of those cheap mood rings I'd had as a child. Half the time, I could predict what colour he'd turn based on his behaviour, but he still managed to surprise me.

A notice appeared on the screen, waiting for me to proceed with the subroutine. I confirmed with a tap on my console. A pre-recorded message echoed through the room, repeated in several languages, including Kyven. The two captives would be hearing the same in their improvised holding cell.

"The ship has been locked down. Fire extermination in progress. Please await further updates. You are safe."

I smiled wryly at the last sentence. That had been my addition after a panicked captive had tried to ram his horns through my wall.

Flicking to the surveillance cameras, I checked on the women. They looked startled and surprised but not terrified or overly suspicious. Hopefully, they'd really think that there was a fire that I had to deal with. I made sure the signal dampeners were active, preventing any contact they might seek with their ship, before broadcasting my own message on the only frequency that wasn't blocked.

"Kyven ship, I has your captain. Surrender cargo if you want her return. Do not dare using A-beam to get captain back. You will fail."

I made my voice as deep and serious as I could.

"You will fail," Aba echoed ominously just before I ended the transmission.

I grinned at him. "That will give them a nice riddle. They'll assume I'm not the only person on board."

"Not the only person."

"Yes, that's right, you're almost a person. Now let's see what they'll reply."

I leaned back in my chair and watched the Kyvens. The woman whose name I didn't know was sitting on the floor, seemingly relaxed, while the captain was pacing back and forth. The space they were locked in was only about five metres long, enough to give her freedom to pace but not enough to let them see much of the ship. Hopefully, they didn't have to stay in there for long. I'd once had someone piss themselves, of course during the one month that my cleaning bot had been broken. I shuddered at the memory.

No answer yet. I double-checked my transmitter. It was working, so they should have received my message. Didn't they want their captain back? One of my nightmare scenarios was coming across a mutinous ship that was happy to have their captain removed from power. Then I'd have to deal with them...somehow. I was not a violent person. I didn't do this because I enjoyed it. I'd never chosen this life. It had been forced on me, and now there was no way back.

[4]

ELLABEE

Something wasn't right. We'd been here for hours, and there hadn't been another update concerning the fire. If that fire had ever even existed.

I looked around the entrance bay that Ja'lal and I were locked in, not that there was much to see. It was mostly just an empty hold with two sealed doors on either side. I knew some ships had emergency protocols, but the Xcruiser174 wasn't one of them. Maybe it had been modified, but still, it shouldn't lock the hatches like that.

"Is this normal?" I asked Ja'lal.

She shook her head. "No, it's not. Not for a ship this size anyway."

Just like I suspected. I knew we should've been

more careful in our approach, but all my caution had gone when I'd seen a single Kyvenoid that looked suspiciously like Heather from Earth Planet. As good as Heather was with wrangling rashipis and other flock animals, she was pretty fragile. From the stories I'd heard, they periodically needed self-induced hibernation and they couldn't survive a simple disembowelment. Any Kyven youngling could regrow their bowels, but not these humans.

Still, I shouldn't have underestimated anyone commandeering a ship, regardless of size. This was definitely my mistake.

I ran my hands over the locked doors, trying to figure out what kind of system we were dealing with here. It was solid, though, with no way for us to get through it.

"What do you think is happening out there?" Ja'lal asked, the concern evident in her voice.

"Probably a misunderstanding," I replied, checking the other hatch that led into the ship. This one was different. It was a different model and much older. Some of the hinges were exposed and I gestured for Ja'lal to come and check them out.

She understood instantly and balled her fist, delivering four forceful strikes against the steel. The material cracked and the doors opened with a hiss, allowing us further entry into the ship. It seemed foolish to go in deeper when we had no idea where that would lead us, but I wasn't going to let some Kyvenoid trap me.

I didn't expect to find a small living space on the other end of the hatch. It was messy and filled with all kinds of junk, but it looked lived in. There were even attempts at making it nice and personalised. Pictures on the wall, some pillows, little trinkets. That made the whole situation only more confusing.

If this Kyvenoid was trying to trap us, why would she do it in her home? Maybe this was all a big misunderstanding.

A buzz sounded and a hatch on the opposite side of the living area opened. Instead of the Kyvenoid, a blue head appeared. Atina.

"What happened?" I asked, quickly making my way over to her. I was keen to get out of here.

She helped me out. "We captured the human and Inil disabled the safety mechanism. It was easy, there's just one of her."

What a weird situation. I had so many questions, but I wasn't going to make the mistake of going in blind this time.

"Get the ship ready for take-off," I told Atina. "We're not staying here any longer than necessary."

"And the human?"

"We take her with us. I want answers, but I'll get them someplace where I'm in control," I commanded. I was going to find out what the human's ulterior motives were. "Where's the human now?"

Atina gestured behind her. "Katak and Estaniu are holding her. She was easy to overpower."

I made my way over to the human who was

stubbornly fighting her restraints. I took another good look at her. She had a similar skin colour to Heather and the same rounded shells of her ear, but her hair was the dark brown of the honglui tree. Her amber eyes glistened with intelligence and anger but I could deal with that. She wasn't the first person to look at me that way.

A strange calm came over me now that I was back in control. "Who are you?"

"Screw you," she spat.

What a weird name, but Heather had said many times that they had strange customs on their Earth Planet.

"Why did you trick us?" I asked.

Screyu gave me a withering stare. "Let me go."

"Take her to the ship. Put her in a cargo bay," I instructed Katak.

With a nod, the two males pulled the human towards the PoTA-2. With a last glance at her small ship, I followed. This whole thing was confusing, but I wasn't going to let one measly female foil me.

We got back to our ship and they took the human away. I returned to the bridge with Atina who got settled in her cockpit while Lini reconnected himself to the ship's mainframe. If we made haste, we could be out of Planet Tarrop's atmosphere and back on course in a few clicks.

"C-Captain?" Lini said with a faint voice. "I'm sorry."

"What?" I joined him by the command panel,

where a host of red lights flickered. "No, what's happening?"

"I think I caught a virus from the cruiser," Lini said, turning around to give his brother access. "Performing full scan of PoTA-2."

I couldn't breathe while I waited for the results. A virus sounded nasty, and without Lini to help navigate the ship, we were almost guaranteed an accident. It was possible to fly manually without him but not for long and certainly not on unfamiliar routes. That was asking to get hit by a stray asteroid or something.

Inil opened his mouth, revealing the lack of teeth. "Full scan complete. PoTA-2's security changed. Permission to take-off not granted."

"What? Override it, I'm the captain."

"Attempting to override. Attempt failed."

I couldn't believe my ears. This was a real issue. If we didn't have permission to launch, we were stranded. And it was all my fault.

The thought of staying on this cursed planet any longer made me want to punch something. Or someone. I'd been wrong. This wasn't my fault. It was the human's. Screyu. If we were stranded here, I'd use that time to have a long, hard chat with her. That female was going to regret ever trying to trick us.

"While we were trapped, what did she say? What did she want?" I asked my crew.

Atina huffed with annoyance. "Our cargo. She wasn't more specific than that."

"I doubt she took the time to research our ship. No,

she's done this before. Lures well-meaning vessels to her, then blackmails them to hand over their cargo. What a way to make a living. Well, this stops today. I won't have her do this to anyone else. I will interrogate her now, but in the meantime, contact the Intergalactic Authorities. They can pick her up from here, or we can drop her off at their nearest patrol station."

Lini turned to me, and I knew what he was going to say before he could open his mouths. "The virus has affected our transmission equipment. We can't send messages at the moment."

I groaned. "How long until it's fixed?"

"Unknown."

Inil and Lini weren't a species that were known for their imagination. They wouldn't give me guesses, only hard facts. Some days, I valued that straight-talking ability, but today, I would have appreciated a bit of hope.

"Alright, let me know once you have an estimate. I want to contact the authorities as soon as possible. I'll be with our prisoner if you need me."

Satisfied that my crew were working their hardest to restore the ship's systems, I hurried to the cargo bay. Estaniu was standing guard outside a shipping container, which he and Katak must have fashioned into an impromptu prison cell. He straightened when he saw me approach.

"Has she said anything?" I asked before peering through the little hatch in the container. The female was sitting at the back of her metal prison, her legs crossed in a funny fashion, seemingly relaxed.

"Yes, but none of it made any sense. I was about to ask Atina's mate to come here and translate for me. She's the same species as this one, isn't she?"

Not a bad idea, but I knew that Screyu spoke enough Kyven to communicate with me. She likely had a translation implant fitted as well; barely anyone travelled through space nowadays without one. Maybe her broken Kyven earlier had all been an act, just like everything else. Anger filled me as I looked at how relaxed she was. She was costing me valuable time and credits by delaying us from our next stop. The least she could do was show some regret for her actions.

"Open the door," I commanded. "I'm going to have a chat with her."

Estaniu hesitated. "Are you sure? She might be dangerous."

I pulled my disembowelment stick from my belt. I didn't like to use it, but sometimes, I didn't have a choice. With this female, I might even enjoy it.

"I'll be fine. Open the door."

This time, he didn't object. I ducked into the container and waited for Estaniu to close the door behind me. He continued to watch us through the hatch. Unnecessary. I hadn't become a ship's captain by being nice and soft. I could handle myself, especially against a feeble human.

Screyu looked up at me but didn't change her

posture. Her expression was blank and guarded. I stayed standing, looking down at her sternly.

"Are you going to torture me? It's not going to work."

I realised I still held the disembowelment stick in my left hand. I put it back in its holster and crossed my arms instead.

"I'm not going to torture you."

"Oh?" She seemed surprised. "Then why am I here?"

How stupid was this human? "You tried to steal my cargo. Did you think we'd just let you carry on? You're not a very smart thief."

"Pirate," she corrected automatically.

"What's the difference?"

She crossed her arms in front of her chest. How many limbs could she cross at once? "It's a lifestyle."

"That lifestyle ends today. We're handing you to the authorities. But first, you're going to answer my questions."

"You said you weren't going to torture me."

What was wrong with her? She seemed rather obsessed with torture. Maybe she was into it. I knew some species enjoyed experiencing pain and humiliation. I hadn't realised humans were one of them.

"I will ask questions and you will answer. Easy. What's so hard to understand about that?"

"What if I don't want to answer?"

"Then..."

I tried to come up with a threat that didn't include disembowelment. She wouldn't survive that.

"Then I will destroy your ship. I'm sure you have things on there you don't want to lose."

Her expression stayed unreadable. She didn't reply, but I could see her mind race behind her beautiful bright eyes. Their colour reminded me of something, but I wasn't quite sure what.

When she didn't say anything, I leaned against the door. "First, why is your Kyven suddenly flawless?"

Screyu didn't answer immediately; I assumed she was assessing whether I could use her response against her. Finally, she shrugged. "I'm using my implant. I didn't know what species your crew are, so I didn't want to rely on my language skills alone."

"So you really do speak some Kyven?"

"Yes."

"How many languages do you know?"

That wasn't something I'd planned to ask, but I was curious. Kyven was a fairly small and unimportant planet on the galactic scale, so it was a strange coincidence that she happened to speak my language.

"Six more or less fluently. I understand at least five more." She sounded both proud and defiant at once.

Against my better knowledge, I was fascinated. Most beings relied on implants to communicate; very few ever bothered to learn other languages. Some did it as a challenge, others to prove their intellect. I wondered what Screyu's motivation had been.

"How did you learn that many?"

"By listening." She spat out the words as if they tasted bad. "I want some food."

"We're not done yet."

"Then ask proper questions."

That she could have. "How long have you been robbing ships?"

"Define robbing."

"You know what robbing is."

"Do I?"

I pushed down the anger bubbling up in me. This woman was doing something to me. She knew exactly what levers to pull. She was manipulating me even now. I wouldn't have that.

"Just answer my question," I snapped.

"I want something to eat first."

"You'll get something to eat when you tell me how you infected Lini and Inil."

She gave me a vacant look. "Ah, the green data twins? Well, that's their fault for hacking into my ship's system. That's very rude, you know? And technically, against the laws of the Galactic Union. I could report you for that."

Her comment made me bristle. She was annoyingly right about that. I felt the urge to poke her a little with the disembowelment stick, but she looked like she might enjoy it. Besides, it would be admitting that she was getting under my skin.

“I'll be back,” I declared stiffly.

The human waved in a manner I'd seen Heather do and had the nerve to smile. “I'll be here.”

Infuriating. Positively infuriating.

[5]

GEORGIA

It was impossible to tell how long I'd been in the cargo bay jail, but from my rumbling stomach, I had to guess close to half a day. It was chilly in here, but not nearly as cold as these bays could go. At some point, a guard had thrown both a bottle of water and an empty container into the cell, which I assumed was to be my toilet for my stay here.

The entrance swung open and the captain walked in again with a bowl. "I brought food."

I expected a bowl of vile ship guts or something, but she presented me with a plate that had actual recognisable chunks of meat and plants. A strange meal for a hostage. Then again, everything about this capture was strange. There'd been no poking or prodding, no slapping or cutting. No touching... Those captors were easily the worst.

The captain put the food down in front of me. "Here, eat."

"Is it poisoned?" I asked.

She gave me a weird look. "No, why would I bring you food to poison you? I want answers first."

I accepted the plate and gave it a tentative sniff. My stomach practically roared and it took everything I had in me not to devour it. I handed it back. "I'm not hungry."

"But you asked for food."

"I wanted to see if you would," I replied cheekily, feeling a rush when I could see the annoyance on the captain's face. For a Kyven, she was very expressive. That made this much easier for me.

The captain surprised me by sitting down on the other side of the bay. "You infected our data specialist."

"They shouldn't have hacked into my ship."

"I want the anti-virus. I know you have it," she said, her voice strained.

She must be mad that I infected her specialist, they always were. Most of these ships were useless without an operator, the downfall of their advanced technology. Nothing was manual any more.

I looked away, something that was bound to infuriate her, but I wasn't scared. And even if I was, I refused to show fear. I'd promised myself long ago that I'd never show weakness to these brutes. Besides, there wasn't anything they could do to me that I hadn't already endured.

"And what if I won't give the anti-virus to you?" I

taunted, studying my fingernails. I wasn't sure if my disinterest translated properly, but it made me feel better.

She barely reacted, just raised her eyebrows with mild confusion. "Why wouldn't you give it to me? I presume you want to trade the cure; otherwise, what's the point of infecting him?"

Oh, she was a clever one.

"You're right. Here's what's going to happen. You're going to let me out of here, you're going to give me your cargo, then I'll fly away. When I'm far enough, I'll give you the cure."

"And why would we believe that?"

"You'll just have to trust me," I said with a smirk.

She shook her head. "That's not an option. You're going to give us the cure, and we'll all go our separate ways without anyone losing their bowels."

Did she really think she was in a position to bargain?

"I'm not giving you the cure first."

The captain crossed her arms firmly across her chest. "You're not in a position to negotiate."

"No, you're mistaken. *You*'re not in a position to negotiate. If you don't let me go, you'll never be able to start your ship, and you'll be stranded here. Are you familiar with this planet? There's not a lot of food around here. If you don't do what I want, you and your entire crew will become nice little gravestones."

I could tell from the clear frustration on her face that she knew I had a point. That was the beauty of my ruse, it never failed. They would soon understand that there was no way to cure their operator without my anti-virus and cave.

The captain ate some of the food from the plate she brought, chewing thoughtfully.

My stomach rumbled again, the traitorous thing. Part of me wished I'd accepted the food after all, but I refused to be bribed and tricked with food.

"Why are you doing this?" she asked, offering the plate to me again.

I ignored it. "Because I'm out of supplies."

"It would've been easier to go to the store," she remarked dryly.

I couldn't help but chuckle. I didn't realise Kyvens had a sense of humour. Or maybe she was serious. I didn't know, but it was funny. Then again, that could be from sitting in this cell. Being locked up always made my brain do funny things.

"What's funny?" the captain asked.

"You."

"Me?" She seemed genuinely confused.

I didn't blame her. I was probably unlike anything or anyone she ever met. There weren't many humans in space, if any. I certainly had never countered another, but then again, I tended to avoid humans. They were just as cruel and awful as the aliens, especially now that I was an outsider.

She seemed to realise that she was showing weakness by so openly displaying her confusion. Her expression hardened, closing off all emotion other than anger. Yes, she was angry at me for refusing her food. Good. I knew how to deal with that. Anger, fury, aggression, threats. It was part of my routine. Kindness confused me. I'd not had to deal with kindness ever since I'd been abducted from Earth. The last kind smile...

I forced myself to focus. "Let me know when you're ready to accept the deal."

The captain glared at me. "I think a few days without food might change your mind. Tell the guard once you're willing to talk again."

She knocked on the door without sparing me another glance. For some reason, I smiled. They always did this. Threatened me with violence, starvation, whatever their twisted minds could conjure. But in the end, when they realised that there was no way to fix their operators without my anti-virus, they changed their tune. They always did, no matter how brutal and ruthless they were in the beginning. I could handle pain and a few days without food.

I watched the door close behind her and made myself comfortable, thinking of all the cargo I'd soon possess. I'd be able to go a few months without having to steal.

A whiff of something hit my nose and I realised she'd left the bowl of food. Intentional or not? I didn't care. I grabbed the bowl and ate as slowly as I could, savouring every bite.

[6]

ELLABEE

The captive confused me to no end. I paced up and down my living quarters, occasionally glancing at the screen to my right to check on the female. She still sat cross-legged, the empty bowl next to her. She'd been hungry. For a moment, it pained me to think that I was planning to deprive her of food, but then I reminded myself of why she was in the makeshift cell. She was my enemy. She'd threatened not just my life, but also that of Ja'lal while we'd been on her crashed vessel, and now my entire crew and ship. I didn't know why I was even tempted to feel pity towards her. It was none of my business that she was painfully thin. Nor should the haunted look in her eyes affect me.

A gong announced someone outside my door.

"Come in!"

Heather hesitantly stepped into the room. Had she ever been in my quarters before? Unlikely. I saw the human every day, but her mate was always around. I could count the times we'd had a conversation without Atina on one hand. But today, I needed her expertise.

"She's human!" Heather exclaimed, her gaze fixed on my screen. "Where did she come from? How did she end up in space? This shouldn't be possible!"

"I don't know," I admitted. "But I'm intending to find out. She is not being very cooperative, however. I need to know more about your species. She refuses to hand me the anti-virus we require to leave this planet. I have to find out her weak spots. Her pressure points. What can I threaten her with that will have an effect?"

Heather didn't stop looking at the female. "How can she be here? She looks too young to be a professional astronaut and even if she was, NASA hasn't even sent people to Mars yet. We're far from anywhere our probes have reached. She must have been abducted by aliens."

"Does that happen often?" I asked curiously.

"There are a lot of people saying that they've been abducted, but until I met Atina, I always assumed they're just crackpots and lunatics. Or people wanting attention, so they make up a ridiculous story. Now, I could imagine that some of those stories were true. Still, I doubt it happens frequently. The authorities would notice."

I hadn't considered just how unusual it was for a human to have her own spaceship. Maybe I should investigate how she came to get it. If I discovered more about her past, I could use it to break this stalemate and find a peaceful solution.

"Since we don't have any live cargo on board just now, I will assign you a new task," I told Heather. "I will research this human and you will help me interpret our findings. I realise I don't know as much about your kind as I should."

"Can I talk to her?"

"No," I said automatically before I could even think about it. Why did I not want Heather to meet the human? What was I worried about? "Not yet," I said more slowly. "If our research is unsuccessful, you or I will talk to her. But first, we will dig into her past and find out everything there is to know about this pirate."

The bridge would be busy with activity, so I decided to work from my quarters instead. I had a spare console for Heather to use, although I let her get us some drinks and snacks first. My gaze was pulled to the screen again. Screyu had her eyes closed, looking more relaxed than she should.

"I will figure you out," I whispered, a promise to both her and me. It was unnerving how undisturbed she looked. It made me wonder if she had something else up her sleeve, like the transmitted virus when we hacked into her ship's control. This was so frustrating.

A loud crash and raised voices came from outside and I got up to see what the ruckus was about. Two of my crew members arrived at my quarters carrying a large cage with the colourful bird that had accompanied the human earlier.

"We got the animal," Griach said, slight smoke coming from the spouts on his head. "But he's wily."

As to prove his point, the bird let out a wild shriek and flapped his wings, making the blue feathers change into a fierce pink. He turned his four eyes to me and hissed from his bright orange beak.

If he was trying to intimidate me, I'd faced bigger and badder.

"Put him inside my cabin," I told the crew, stepping aside so they could bring the bird in. I wasn't sure yet what the significance of him was, but I'd seen before just how much these humans valued their animal companions. Even if I couldn't get anything useful out of the bird, maybe I could use him as leverage.

The crew members pushed the cage inwards, and the bird let out desperate calls. I hated having to keep him locked up, but there was too much on the line to be kind.

I waited before they were gone before I directed my attention to the bird. He glared back at me with a fierceness that felt similar to Screyu. As far as I was aware, these kinds of birds weren't sentient or particularly intelligent, but even from one look, there was something different about this one.

He let out a garble of gibberish sounds and threw himself against the cage. I winced at the sheer force and quickly tossed some ship biscuits at him, hoping that would settle him down. It only seemed to enrage him more and he trampled the biscuits with his talons, stomping them into smithereens.

"Guess you're not hungry then," I said to him.

He gave me a loathing look and spread his wings as far as the cage allowed.

"Wow! He's big!" a voice said from behind me. It was Heather returning with snacks and drinks.

The bird echoed the sound and this time, I registered it as one of the Earth languages. My translator implant must not have been dialled in properly. Then again, why would it? It was an animal and as far as I knew, this variety wasn't capable of communicating with the locals.

"Did he just repeat what you said?" I asked Heather, wanting to make sure I wasn't going crazy.

The human dropped the snacks on the nearby table. "He did. That's neat! It's like a parrot."

"Parrot, parrot!" the bird repeated.

"What's a parrot?" I asked, the word foreign to me.

"It's a specific type of bird that can repeat sounds and words, like this one." Heather leaned in closer, and the bird visibly relaxed when she spoke.

Interesting. He must like the sound of her voice or find comfort in hearing a familiar language. Now I was extra glad that I'd sent the crew to catch him. If I could get him to talk, maybe he could tell me how to get a cure.

I leaned down to put myself at eye height with his dominant set of eyes. "Tell me about the virus."

The bird just stared at me, a vacant look in his colourful eyes.

Heather let out a hum. "Do you really think he'll know how to cure Lini and Inil?"

"Cure?" the bird echoed almost instantly.

"Yes, cure! Tell me how to cure them!" I shouted at the bird.

He remained quiet again, the little ma'ak.

"I think he can't or won't mimic Kyven. He seems to only be repeating my words," Heather said. "Maybe he only speaks English. That must mean the pirate speaks English, too."

"English! English! Fuck the English!" the bird cried out, proving her theory right, except that he hadn't just repeated her, he'd said more.

“Maybe we can use him to get Screyu to talk,” I mused out loud.

“Screyu?” Heather repeated slowly.

“Yes, the pirate. She introduced herself as that.”

“Oh, I doubt that... ‘Screw you’ is kind of a curse.”

Great, so I didn't even know the pirate's name? That would make it even harder to establish trust, which we were going to need if we were going to resolve this.

I looked back at the monitor where she was sitting against the back of the container, gazing into the distance. She still looked unbothered and carefree, clearly not worried about being deprived of food or her freedom.

This whole thing was heavily bizarre. Not only

were we stranded on a deserted planet, I had a human in captivity and a bird who could speak an Earth language. Or mimic. It wasn't entirely clear.

Suddenly, I wasn't so sure about our approach. Everything we'd done so far was exactly what she wanted, starting from responding to her emergency call to hacking into her ship. She'd planned this all out... And now she just had to wait.

A smarter, less stubborn Kyven would have given in already, but I'd refused to hand all my cargo over. Especially without a guarantee that she would give us the cure once we complied with her wishes. One of us was going to have to bend. The main question was... who?

[7]

GEORGIA

It was hard to estimate how long I'd been in this jail cell, but from past experience, it wouldn't be long until the captain caved. The virus I'd programmed would keep their operator sick, and nobody wanted to be stranded on these planets. No cargo was worth that.

The door opened and it was not a surprise that the captain had returned, her white hair tied up in a typical Kyven braid. She was probably here to make more threats, but there was nothing she could say that could scare me.

She sat down on the other side of the cell. "Let's talk."

"Talk?" I frowned. That was an unusual approach. At this stage, I expected some poking and prodding, maybe a bit of whipping. These aliens liked brute force, but they'd never got close to breaking me. Maybe humans were just more resilient.

"What's your name?" the captain asked, sounding genuinely curious.

"My name doesn't matter."

"It does to me." She opened her mouth in a weird way and wrangled out a vaguely familiar sound. "Englick?"

It took me a moment to register what she meant. "English?"

She nodded. "Englick."

"Englishhh."

"Englisk," she said, the harsh clicking sounds of the Kyven language creeping into the way she pronounced the softer end of the word.

"Close." I only realised I was smiling when she smiled at me. I quickly forced my face back to a neutral expression, refusing to be sucked into whatever weird strategy this was. How did she even know what language I was speaking?

"Where are you from?" the captain asked, switching back to Kyven. "Where on Earth?"

She was probably the first alien I'd ever heard use the English name for my home planet rather than the official designation, #47283. I bet she'd done it on purpose to impress me. Maybe this was her strategy. Rather than violence, she'd try to squirrel the cure out of me by pretending to be nice. I wouldn't fall for it.

"None of your business. How's your navigator?"

For a second, her smile wavered, but then it

returned. She was stunning when she smiled. At first, I'd thought her braided hair was white, but it was actually such a pale shade of blue that it shimmered like silver. Kyvens usually had dark blue hair, so she'd either dyed it, or she was an anomaly. People who were different from the norm usually became outcasts or leaders. In her case, she'd chosen the path to the top. It was hard to guess her age, but I doubted she was much older than me. A young captain, yet clearly in charge, judging from how her crew had followed her orders without hesitation. I almost admired her, but that would lead me down a sticky rabbit hole. I had to remember that she was my enemy. Glancing around my boring metal prison was an easy reminder.

"How did you come to be here?" Ellabee asked instead of answering my snarky question. "How long ago did you leave Earth?"

"Why do you care?"

"You're strange. A mystery. I like to solve mysteries."

I watched her closely for any sign of a lie, but she was purposely being as open as possible. And she was still smiling despite my hostility. It confused me to no end, even though I wouldn't let her see that. Why had she decided to be nice to me?

"Maybe you should focus on curing your navigator," I quipped harshly. "Don't waste your energy on me."

"Are you not worth it?"

That question took me aback. What was I even supposed to say to that? I stayed quiet, glaring at her instead. I wished I had Aba with me. He would have cursed this Kyven in a hundred colourful ways already.

"Where is my bird?" I snapped, ignoring her question. "What did you do to him?"

"What kind of bird is he?"

"Is that all you do? Answering questions with more questions? I have enough of this."

I squiggled around so that my back faced her. It was a risky move, but I couldn't let her see just how much she was unsettling me. I'd lost count of how many ships I'd hijacked, at least two dozen, but their captains had never reacted like this strange woman.

"Now you're being childish," she scolded. "Our conversation isn't over yet."

"You're clearly not interested in answering my questions."

"Neither are you. How about we do a deal? An answer for an answer. We take turns. Honest answers only. I will know if you lie."

Were Kyvens among those dangerous species that could spot a lie? I was pretty sure they weren't, but since I'd had no contact with any Kyvens since my escape from Klen, I wasn't entirely certain. Remembering Ellabee's steel-blue eyes, I could easily imagine her seeing deep into my mind, my soul even. Not that I had a soul, not anymore. All that was left were black scraps of guilt and pain.

"Get us two glasses of honglui juice and some snacks," I heard the captain say to someone outside my cell. "And tell Atina to take control of the bridge. I'll be here for a while."

Footsteps hurried away. Were we left without a guard? Maybe this was an opportunity to escape. Ellabee was taller than me and looked in great shape, but I'd learned some nasty self-defence tricks in the past few years. I could probably take her down before she knew what was happening. But then what? I didn't know where they were holding Aba. I couldn't abandon him. There was no way of searching the ship without getting caught. Fuck. This may be my only opportunity to run, yet here I was, attached to a bloody alien parrot. The irony wasn't lost on me. I was in this situation because of aliens and couldn't get away because, yes, aliens. Aba may not have been particularly clever, but he counted as an alien to me.

"How about you turn around again?" Ellabee said softly. She sounded almost gentle. Without the sharp edge of command, her voice had a soothing quality that made me want to listen to her for hours.

As much as I wanted to resist, this was too good an offer. I'd get answers. And I hadn't agreed to telling the truth. Ellabee had said that, not me. I'd experiment with a few small, insubstantial lies first to see if she could spot them.

Slowly, I turned until I was facing her again. I crossed my arms in front of my chest and glared at the silver-haired woman. In return, she simply smiled. Her patience seemed endless. It made me want to scream with frustration. I preferred my enemies to be dumb, violent, ugly aliens, not beautiful females who smiled at me like nobody had in many, many years. Fuck. I could feel myself softening already by just looking at her. This was unfair.

"How about we start with something simple?" she said with that disarming smile. "What's your name? Your real name."

Did it really matter? It wasn't like she could do anything with that information. But just in case, I'd only give her my first name.

"Georgia."

"She-ooor-sheee-aaaah."

She drew my name like those cheese strings I loved as a child. Did they still have cheese strings on Earth, or had they moved on? As so often before, I realised that my home planet was no longer my home. I'd be a stranger there if I ever found my way back.

"Almost. Geor-gi-a."

Ellabee repeated it again, almost accurately.

"What does it mean?" she asked curiously.

"It's my turn first. Save your question for after. Where is my bird?" I asked, feeling nervous. There weren't many things I cared about, but Aba was one of them. I hoped they weren't mistreating him, or worse, turning him into dinner.

"In my cabin. Don't worry; he's well looked after. Maybe you should tell me what he likes to eat, but I won't waste a question on that." She gave me a piercing stare that made her eyes sparkle in a frustratingly pretty way. "Do you do this often?"

I shrugged. "It's not my first time."

"That's not a real answer."

"You didn't ask the right question. My turn. How are you going to take off without your operator?" I returned, grinning when Ellabee's face fell.

The captain got up from the cell, frustration dancing on her brow, and left without another word. A surge of exhilaration rushed through me, and I basked in the triumph. I might be the one locked up, but I wasn't the one trapped on this planet, and we both knew it.

[8]

ELLABEE

On closer inspection, the small Xcruiser174 wasn't very impressive. It had rust on the sides, which showed it was stationary for a lot of the time and didn't get cleaned or maintained nearly as much as it should. Some of the parts were mismatched, so Georgia clearly didn't visit official ports for repairs. Maybe she even did them herself. That was both dumb and impressive.

I disliked that I was having complimentary thoughts about Georgia, but I had to hand it to the pirate. She was smart and definitely had the attitude of a captain. If we'd met under different circumstances, maybe I'd even like her.

But we hadn't.

The bird croaked from inside his cage and flapped his four wings, hitting them against the metal ribs of his confinement. I felt bad for keeping him locked up like that, but I'd seen Georgia's response. She definitely cared about that animal, and I intended to use it to my advantage.

Two of my crew members came out of the ship and one held up his scanner. "All clear, no hidden traps, but all the systems are encrypted."

"That's okay, I just want to have a look around." I gestured to the bird. "Can you help me bring him inside? I want to see if he'll talk again."

The crew helped me carry the cage into the ship and they departed with a thoughtful nod, leaving me with Georgia's things. Hopefully, something about this would help me figure out how to cure Lini and Inil without having to give in to her blackmail.

I wandered through the main living area of the ship, taking in the sight around me. There was a lot of clutter around that reminded me of something Atina once said about the sentients of Earth. They were a sentimental sort. That much was clear from all the trinkets everywhere, most of which I didn't even recognise.

The bird let out a shrill shriek. "All aboard, all aboard!"

"Yes, we're on board, tell me more," I encouraged him.

He stared at me like I was the one with four eyes.

Right, he didn't understand Kyven.

"Englisk?" I tried, twisting my tongue to make the soft sound at the end.

"English! English! Fuck the English!" he repeated happily.

"Yes, good!" I tried to remember how Georgia pronounced her name. "Georshia?"

The bird's reaction was instant. "Georgia! Georgia is the best!"

I chuckled, amused by him. I could see why she kept him around, especially in a one-man ship.

"Yes, Georshia. Georshiaaa," I drew out, trying to pronounce her name properly.

"Georgia! Georgia? Where are you? Where are you?"

That was a good question and one I wasn't going to answer. But it gave me more of their English words to mimic and hopefully, that could trigger more conversation with the bird. He was certainly more talkative than Georgia and since he could only echo and mimic, maybe I could get something useful out of him.

I picked up a nearby item, some sort of ball on a string, and held it out to the bird.

"Let's play some games! Let's play some games!"

"Gamesh? Plaj?" I echoed, doing my best to recreate the sounds as accurately as I could. It was hard to distinguish his original language while my translator spoke in my head, but I was managing just about.

The bird flapped his wings. "Play! I want to play, but there's nobody to play with."

"Nowboodie."

"Nobody! All alone, all alone! Nobody cares for me!"

I felt my gut twist. These all had to be things that she said to him once, and it made me somehow feel sorry for the pirate holding me and my entire crew hostage. I had to wonder why she'd even resorted to a ruse like this. There had to be easier ways to get supplies and rations than stealing them from other ships. Maybe that was something I could ask her when we spoke next.

With a sigh, I picked up another item, some sort of ticking thing with dials, but I couldn't make out what it was supposed to be either. None of this was going to help me out.

I moved to the control section of the ship and turned the power on, but it was all encrypted like the crew had said. And without Lini, there was definitely no way to break into it. When we got out of here, I was definitely going to hire another one just in case. Or maybe next time, I wouldn't just mindlessly respond to an emergency call no matter what.

"Time to fly!" the bird cawed.

It sounded surprisingly enthusiastic. Was it mimicking Georgia's love of flying, or was that the bird's sentiment? It was hard to tell. I made a mental note to have the PoTA-2's AI compile a report on the animal's species and just how intelligent they were. That would make interpreting its exclamations easier.

"Yes, flaaay," I said in English, hoping to encourage

it to say more. But this time, it only cocked its head, looking at the controls, then at the dark screens in front of us. If the ship hadn't been encrypted, I may have been tempted to take it for a quick spin to see if that would make the bird talk. But as things were, I didn't have a single ship capable of flying. I suppressed a curse. This had to be one of the lowest points of my career. What good was a captain without a functional ship?

"If you're not going to divulge anything else, let's head back."

The bird stared at me, then opened and closed its beak several times before semi-whispering, "Sorry. Sorry."

"Sorry?" I repeated in surprise. Again, I could hear the emotion in his quiet squawk.

"I have to, sorry. I'm sorry."

If I'd had my eyes closed and only heard the bird's voice, I would have sworn it was a sentient apologising for something terrible they'd done. If it was echoing Georgia, then did that mean that she wasn't a pirate out of passion but necessity? Or was it an apology for something else she'd done?

"You're giving me more questions than answers," I complained. "Can't you just tell me what I want to know?"

"Tell, tell, tell."

"Now you're just repeating me."

Its colours changed to bright red. "Me. Good parrot. Clever parrot. Verrrrry good parrot."

"Ugh. I guess it's time to go. I will get more out of Georgia than you."

"Georrrrgia! Georgia is the best!"

I rolled my eyes and grabbed the bird's cage, carrying him carefully back out. If I'd been a crueller person, maybe I would have hurt him to get Georgia to do what I wanted, but that was against my nature. Besides, after hearing him say all these things, I couldn't help but feel sad for Georgia.

When I saw her tomorrow, I would try a different approach.

[9]

GEORGIA

The door to the cell opened and I jolted from my light slumber. It wasn't easy to get good sleep in a place like this, but I'd had worse nights, most of which I owed to my own brain and the nightmares it created.

Captain Ellabee stepped inside with breakfast on a tray - or whatever meal of the day this was. I'd lost track a while ago. She kept threatening to withhold food, but she never did, which was very unusual. Most aliens had no qualms about depriving me of my basic necessities and adding some pain and torture on top. None of that had happened here; the only thing I was lacking was my freedom, but that was to be expected given the circumstances.

"Good morning," she said, handing me the tray without asking questions or making demands.

I frowned, confused about the whole thing. "You're not going to make me work for it?"

"No, I thought we could just talk today."

"Talk?" I almost let out a sneering laugh. She was mistaken if she thought she could take me off guard with a good-cop routine. I could see right through her.

Ellabee nodded and sat down on the other side of the cell. "Maybe I could tell you something about myself first?"

"Be my guest," I returned sarcastically, not even sure if Kyvens even understood sarcasm. They were very direct, so maybe the finer passive-aggressiveness of life would go right over her head.

"I never wanted to be a captain," she said, her voice calm and soft for a Kyven. "I had plans to be a manitara. Do you know what that is?"

"No," I replied, rolling my eyes.

"It's someone who works with credits and accounts."

"An accountant?" I couldn't hold back my surprise. The fierce silver-haired captain in front of me wanted to be an accountant?

Ellabee nodded, a sad look appearing in her eyes. "I'm good with numbers. I was right on track to get my qualifications when my parents astralised and my whole world fell apart."

That word didn't translate either, but I understood what she meant from the sad look in her eyes. There was a kind of pain in them that I recognised from my own look in the mirror, a type of loss that left a hole that could never be filled. I felt sorry for her until I remembered who she was and that she was my captor.

I crossed my arms. "I don't see how any of that is relevant."

"I know what it's like to be lost and alone," she said, her gaze locking with mine. "Just like you are."

It felt strangely intimate, and I quickly looked away. "I'm not lost or alone. I have Aba and we're just fine."

"Aba. Is that the name of your bird?" Ellabee asked.

Shit, I shouldn't have let that slip. The less they knew about me, the better.

Frustrated, I clenched my hands into tight fists. "I don't care about your sad story. When are you going to realise that you won't get off this planet without me giving you the anti-virus? Just hand over your cargo and we can each go our merry way."

Ellabee gave me an indecipherable look. "That's not going to happen. We will crack your system and figure out what you've done to Lini and Inil."

"Good luck with that. Nobody has ever managed it before. Just know that the longer you take, the sicker your operator gets. You don't want to be responsible for their death, do you?" I bluffed. The virus wasn't meant to kill; I wouldn't have any leverage if they died, but they didn't have to know that. As long as they thought it was fatal, that was the main thing. Sooner or later, they all gave in to the pressure.

"Why are you doing this? For the money? Why

don't you just get an honest job instead?" She sounded both curious and exasperated.

I could have told her how it was impossible to be employed as an unregistered alien from an unknown planet. Earth wasn't part of any of the intergalactic treaties that controlled laws, taxes, and other boring stuff, which meant I couldn't legally work. I also couldn't return home, because, money. There were no regular ships bound for Earth and my own little cruiser wasn't powerful enough to make the journey. I once had the AI calculate the chances. It had told me that I had a two per cent probability of reaching the planet alive - within twenty years. I'd decided to use that time to earn enough money to charter a bigger ship instead. Or steal one, if I ever got the chance. Ellabee's ship was certainly big enough for that trip, but it couldn't be flown by a single person. It needed a crew and operators able to link with the interface.

"Why are you smiling?" Ellabee demanded. I hadn't even realised that a smirk had crept across my lips.

"Because you're funny," I said. Just because she didn't get the joke didn't mean it wasn't funny.

"I am not," she bit back.

"Now you sound like a child."

"I... Ah, you're impossible! Infuriating! I don't know why I even bother," she exclaimed.

"Neither do I. Why do you bother? Why do you keep bringing me food even though you threaten to starve me every time we talk?"

"Because it's the decent thing to do," she snapped,

her steel-blue eyes blazing. "Just like it was the right thing to do to follow your distress call. That's what makes this worse. The only people you trap are decent people wanting to help. They don't deserve this. *I* don't deserve this."

My smile froze into something ugly and painful. She was right. I'd had that exact thought many, many times before. And yet I still did it. Because it was the fastest way to get credits, to get home.

Ellabee unceremoniously slammed the food tray on the floor. "I think it's time I go. I'm wasting my time with you."

She turned to leave. I didn't know what made me call for her to stop.

"What?" she snapped.

"How's my bird?"

"Talking too much. Just like you aren't talking enough. I just wish anything he said made sense."

I had to suppress a smile. That was exactly how I felt about Aba. Sometimes I just wanted him to shut up, but at the same time, I was desperate to know what went on in that scaled little head of his.

"Thank you for looking after him," I forced myself to say.

"This is between you and me. He is innocent."

She was so reasonable, so honourable, that for some reason, I felt like crying. Not that I ever cried. I'd stopped that a long time ago. I could fake tears if I felt it would give me an advantage during an interrogation or a torture session, but they weren't real.

Captain Ellabee was confusing me yet again. I reacted to her so very differently from what I was used to. I just couldn't predict what she was going to do next. It both scared and excited me.

"He really likes Avillian groundnuts," I muttered when she once again turned to leave.

She made a choked sound, almost like a chuckle, then the door shut behind her, leaving only silence and my endlessly circling thoughts.

[10]

ELLABEE

Atina's red-haired mate sat on my lounger, looking stiff and uncomfortable. Maybe I should offer for her to work in her own cabin if she didn't like being in mine.

I took a seat at the table, careful not to disturb the snoozing bird too much. It half opened one eye, blinked at me, then seemed to decide that I wasn't worth waking up for and continued sleeping.

"Have you found anything?" I asked Heather.

"Yes. How do I get this to show on the big screen?"

I took the tablet from her and sent the data to my viewscreen. A picture of a human girl caught my eye among all the alien text. Was that...?

"I managed to access a British database of missing people," Heather said, pride shimmering in her voice. "No idea how I can even get that information from space, but I'm glad I was able to. There are only five girls named Georgia that have gone missing in the past few decades, but going by age, ethnicity and hair colour, this one looks like the one. Georgia Stockwood disappeared without a trace the day after her fifteenth birthday. She disappeared from a village not far from mine, actually. They interviewed all sorts of suspects, but nobody was ever charged with her kidnapping."

"She looks about fifteen, so her abduction can't have been long ago," I mused.

Heather looked at me strangely, then chuckled. "For a moment I forgot that Kyven years are different from ours. Earth years are shorter, so fifteen means she wasn't even an adult yet. I can't remember the exact calculation, but I think it was about times 1.8 to get from Kyven to Earth age. I'd have to ask my cousin; she will know."

"Oh. How old does she look to you?"

"Maybe mid-twenties? That would mean she's been away from Earth for ten years." Heather's eyes widened. "Wow, poor girl. I can't imagine what she must have been through..."

I couldn't help but peek at the small screen showing Georgia in her cell. She'd curled up on the floor, her face hidden under her unruly hair. She'd just become even more intriguing. To have been taken from a backwater planet like Earth and thrust into life in space... it was a miracle she was still alive.

I forced myself to focus back on Heather. "What else did you find?"

"Not much. I was about to look into her ship, where it came from and who it used to belong to when you came back. Want me to continue?"

"No, I'll take it from here. I need you and Atina to check the Xcruiser174 and see if you can figure out the encryption."

Heather gave me a worried look. "I'll try, but I can't make any promises. I know how to google, but I don't have a clue about spaceships."

"Yes, but if you're from the same area and speak Englisk, maybe you'll find a way in," I reasoned, hoping that she would. If we couldn't get into the system, we'd have no choice but to give in to her demands before Lini and Inil perished.

She nodded. "Okay, I'll do that. If you need any more help, let me know."

"Need help, need help," the bird echoed sleepily. For some reason, I thought he sounded relieved.

Once Heather was gone, I got to work to retrace Georgia's steps. Every ship came with its own identification code and registration. While I couldn't access that, some of the parts she used to make repairs had their own serial numbers, and those could be tracked.

I fed the digits into the database, one of the few servers we could still use. I didn't fully understand how the virus worked, but it seemed to block all outgoing communications but allowed some in. I didn't know if that was by accident or on purpose, but I was going to take advantage of it to find out as much as I could about Georgia.

I got a hit on one of the serial numbers that were from a batch that had gone missing a good while ago. The article claimed that they lost the parts in a fire during transit, but I knew that was code for saying they got stolen. No captain liked to admit they were robbed, and if I was forced to hand my cargo over to Georgia, I'd concoct my own story to explain it to our clients. It was hard enough to get return customers; I didn't need them thinking I was incompetent.

Curious, I checked the timestamp and calculated that this had happened shortly after she was abducted from her planet. That proved she'd been doing this for a long time. It made me wonder what exactly happened and why she hadn't tried returning to her home planet.

Or maybe she had. I tried to put myself in her situation. She had neither family nor friends nor crew to help her. She'd been taken from her home and thrust into a world she didn't understand. She would have had no money when she'd been abducted. And no one to turn to.

The thought made me angry. Whoever had taken her may still be out there. I should try and find out their name from Georgia. Maybe I could alert the authorities. As much as my throatfilters itched with the urge to take the abductors on myself, I couldn't endanger my crew for a personal vendetta.

Huh. Personal. For some reason, I felt like I had to protect Georgia. That made no sense at all. That female had broken my ship and my operators. Inil and Lini were still fighting the virus and had to be under constant medical and technical supervision. I should take Georgia to the authorities, not worry about whoever had abducted her.

I realised I was fiddling with my braids, a clear sign that I was agitated. I'd thought I'd shaken that annoying habit a while ago. Luckily, there was nobody to witness my momentary loss of composure. The bird had its head tucked underneath one wing. What had Georgia said? Aba liked Avillian groundnuts. I should see if we had any on board. That might get it to divulge some more useful information. But for now, I had to focus on the task at hand.

After entering another fifty or so serial numbers, I was convinced that Georgia's ship was only held together by luck and bravery. It seemed almost every part of it had been stolen, then used and reused in various ways. She'd even repurposed a food processor chip to keep the main engine running. It was both genius and an accident waiting to happen. How she'd not crashed for real was a miracle. And I didn't even believe in miracles.

I couldn't help but admire the female. She was clearly more intelligent than I'd given her credit for. She wouldn't have had any formal training in technology, not at the age she'd been abducted, so she must have taught herself how to operate her cruiser. I now saw both the ship and its owner with new eyes.

"Shooorshhhhie," the bird suddenly muttered into

its feathers, startling me. I stared at it, but it kept its head under its wing, clearly still asleep. It took me a moment to understand what it had said. Georgie. Aba missed its owner.

My hearts hurt a little as I watched the bird sleep. As much as I hated being caught by Georgia, I hated being her captor even more. Maybe it was time to accept that this stalemate had gone on long enough and cut her loose. I'd walk away without cargo and a serious dent in my pride, but at least I wouldn't be another bad guy in her story.

[11]

GEORGIA

The doors to the cargo bay opened wide and Ellabee came in with a determined expression. I'd seen that look before. That was usually when they decided they were done playing nice.

I fought against my body's reflexes to curl into a ball. I wasn't scared, and there was nothing she could take from me that hadn't been taken before.

She tossed me something and a bundle of metal landed in my lap. Cuffs.

I frowned, surprise flitting through me. "What's that for?"

"You've been in here for a while. I'm betting you miss the sun."

"I don't. The sun is too harsh for me," I replied

casually, refusing to let her know just how desperate I was to be outside again.

"Fresh air then."

It was physically painful to keep my body still and not dash out like an eager puppy. I couldn't let my guard down, no matter how much the promise of fresh air was tempting me. This was all a game to make me compliant and grateful and break me.

"It's not that fresh," I countered, biting the inside of my cheek so I didn't forget that she was my enemy. They all were. Humans, aliens, all of them were capable of hurting me.

Ellabee rolled her eyes, a gesture I'd never seen any Kyven do. "Just get up so we can go for a walk? Unless you'd rather stay here."

This was definitely a trick, but I wouldn't say no to the opportunity to escape or stretch my legs. I put the cuffs on but didn't lock them properly. I couldn't leave the planet without Aba, but it would be preferable if I wasn't in their custody.

I crossed the cell to the entrance where Ellabee blocked my path. I gave her an innocent look. "What?"

She gestured to my arms. "I want to check the cuffs."

Not surprising. I lifted my hands up and she took them in hers, her touch surprisingly gentle. Her blue fingers travelled up my wrist and a tingle ran up my arms from where she examined me. Her hands were strong and the six fingers didn't look nearly as odd as when I'd first seen them. The way they moved together was slightly mesmerising, and I forgot what she was doing until they reached the cuffs. She tugged on the metal and clicked them together properly when she realised they were only half on.

I gave her my best disarming smile. "Oops, I must not have put them on correctly. I don't go around cuffing myself."

She just hummed and nodded towards the exit. "Let's go."

It felt surreal that I was walking out of the cell without a single scratch or even a rumbling stomach. I had no doubt I'd be back here when she didn't get what she wanted from me but as far as captivity went, this had been the easiest few days ever.

Two crew members were waiting outside as well, but they ignored me, clearly just standing guard. I had a good look around and realised I was being kept in the cargo bay, which was kind of ironic given the nature of my request. Ellabee gestured for me to follow her to the open loading dock and on our way out, I marvelled at the vast quantities of holds and bays. I could only guess what they contained, but this was going to be a good haul for me.

I descended the ramp and held my hands up to shield my eyes from the sun. It was still early, but the weather seemed lovely. The soft breeze was even better; it played with my hair and tickled my skin. If it wasn't for my cuffed hands, it would've felt like freedom.

Ellabee let out a little smug chuckle. "Knew you'd like the outside."

I felt like giving a clever retort, but I was enjoying the moment too much. I wasn't going to let her take that away from me. I was sure it wouldn't be long until I was soaring through the stars again and enjoying sunrises on my own time, but I never took the future for granted. This could be the last thing I saw before Ellabee did unspeakable things to me, although it seemed unlikely.

A caw drew my attention and I turned, my heart soaring when two crew members were pushing a large cage outside. Aba flapped his wings when he saw me and whistled a happy tune.

"Aba!" I hurried towards my bird and attempted to stick my hands through the bars, but my cuffs didn't let me.

"Aba! Aba! Aba!" he echoed happily.

"No, you dumb bird, I'm Georgia."

"Georgia! Georgia! My name is Georgia!" He pressed his head against the bars so I could tickle him with a finger. "That's the spot!"

I laughed at his silliness until I remembered where I was and why we were separated in the first place. Ellabee was watching me with a weird look on her face, and I suddenly felt weirdly vulnerable, more so than when she had me locked up in the cell. It dawned on me that she'd done this to catch me off guard. Now I'd shown her just how much I loved this stupid bird.

My mouth turned ashen at the realisation and I felt

like crying, a sensation I hadn't had in years. I refused to show weakness, so I turned away from Aba, ignoring his happy cawing. For his safety, it was better to pretend I didn't care, although I wasn't sure if she would still believe that.

"You really care about that bird," Ellabee said. It wasn't a question. It was a statement.

"I'm raising him for slaughter," I lied, although she clearly didn't believe me.

She shook her head dismissively. "Everyone has something they care about. I'm tired of this stalemate. We're going to negotiate and come to a solution before this gets even more out of hand, understood?"

A chill ran up my spine. I'd heard plenty of pleas, threats and curses, but this was different. This was a command, and from the steel look in her eyes, I knew this was the best offer I was going to get.

"What do you have to offer besides the cargo that I will get one way or another?" I challenged. The two or three times I had been in this situation previously, my captors would threaten me with taking my life or my limbs. I should have known that Ellabee was going to be different.

"Passage to your home planet."

I didn't understand at first. Her lips moved, but the words didn't seem to enter my ears at the same time. Or maybe my brain just didn't process them. It took me several seconds to get the message and even then, I wasn't sure if I'd misheard.

"What?"

"I can take you to planet #47283, also known as Earth. That's where you're from, right?"

She was toying with me. She had to. She was dangling this beautiful, gorgeous carrot in front of me and as soon as I tried to take a bite, she'd jank it back. I knew I wouldn't be able to deal with the disappointment.

"You're bluffing. Nobody ever flies to Earth. It's not on any of the trade routes. It would probably cost you more in fuel than your cargo is worth."

Ellabee's piercing blue gaze moved to something behind me. "Heather, would you join us?"

I swirled around only to be faced with the first human I'd seen in ten long, lonely years.

I'd have rubbed my eyes if my hands hadn't been cuffed. The woman in front of me was slightly older than me, freckles dotted all over a pale face that was framed by beautiful ginger hair. With her faded t-shirt revealing impressive arm muscles, she looked like someone who didn't shy away from physical work.

She smiled at me, a smile that reached all the way to her eyes.

I didn't return the smile. Instead, I faced Ellabee again, fuming.

"A hologram? You're trying to trick me. Nice try. But there's no way there's an actual human here."

"I'm real," the hologram said in a kind voice. "I know it will be hard to believe, but you're not the only woman who has met aliens and travelled through space."

I refused to look at her again. She was just an

illusion. Ellabee wasn't playing fair, that meant I didn't have to, either. Negotiating my arse. She wasn't interested in it at all. She just wanted to explore my weaknesses and take advantage of them. But I wouldn't let her. She was going to regret this. I was going to make her pay.

[12]

ELLABEE

This wasn't going as planned. I'd imagined Georgia to be happy, grateful even when she met Heather. Instead, she stared at me as if I'd physically hurt her. I wasn't sure how to react. Whenever I tried to be nice to her, she misunderstood my intentions.

"Georgia," Heather said softly.

Maybe I should tell the human to leave. I didn't want her to get hurt in case our captive let go of the fury shimmering in her eyes. Georgia was in cuffs, but I'd learned not to underestimate her.

"I will show you that I'm not a hologram," Heather continued. Before I could stop her, she stepped closer to Georgia and hugged her.

Stars. This had been a bad idea. Atina would hold me personally responsible if something happened to her mate. I may have been the captain, but I wasn't immune to mutinies.

I was about to pull the two females apart when I heard the tiniest whisper from Georgia.

"You're real."

Looking over Georgia's shoulder, Heather gave me a meaningful look. I stepped back to let this unforeseen situation unfold, although my muscles were tense, ready to jump in if necessary. The redhead held my captive in a gentle but close embrace.

Something cold and bitter stirred in my belly, a feeling I'd never experienced. For a moment, I wanted to tear them apart, making sure that Heather stopped touching Georgia. I crossed my arms in front of my chest to stop myself from doing anything stupid. Whatever this feeling was, I could conquer it. Besides, why would I even want to touch the captive? She was a pirate, a gorgeous pirate, yes, but in the end she was just a criminal.

"You're real," Georgia repeated slowly. "How?"

"I can tell you my full life story later, but for now, all you have to know is that I am human, that I'm here by my own free will, and that Captain Ellabee wants to help you."

I mentally cursed her for saying the last bit. She'd revealed too much. It wouldn't help in the negotiations, if we ever got to that stage.

"Where are you from?" Georgia asked.

Heather replied with an Englisk word that sounded

like gibberish to me, but it Georgia seemed to recognise it.

"Were you also taken by the Ska'av? Did they experi-"

"No," Heather said quickly. "Long story, but I was taken by my cousin's mate. It wasn't against my will, not really. Well, I didn't know we'd end up living on an alien planet, but Tamsia never really lied to us. She just didn't give us the full truth."

"The Ska'av?" I interrupted their chatter. "I thought they were a myth. Did they abduct you?"

Heather gently let go of Georgia, making that coldness in my belly abate a little. The pirate looked at me, her confused expression betraying a storm of emotions. She was vulnerable just now. I could have taken advantage of that, but I didn't want to. If half of the things I'd heard about the Ska'av were true, this female had suffered more than anyone ever should.

"They did," she replied, her voice flat but her eyes swimming with turmoil.

"How did you escape?"

"They sold me when I got too old for their personal taste to a rich but dumb alien that I killed on my way out." The way she relayed the facts was detached, like she was recalling someone else's story, not her own past.

Now I felt even worse for taking her captive, although she'd forced my hand in the way she'd orchestrated the whole situation. But hopefully, we'd be able to move forward now that I'd extended this offer. It would only work if she wanted to return to

Earth but from the way she reacted, I would bet she did.

Georgia stared at me, her hands still clenched tightly. From what I'd learned about their species, this wasn't good.

Heather sensed it too, and reached out to Georgia, touching her shoulder in what seemed to be a soothing gesture. I grimaced seeing it but also committed it to memory. If I was going to get along with Georgia, I'd have to learn these things. I didn't know why it mattered to me, but the more I learned about the human female, the more I felt compelled to help her. Even if she was treating me like her enemy.

"If you have any more questions, I'd be happy to answer them later," Heather said in a tone she normally used to calm down the rashipis when they got too rowdy. It seemed to work on our pirate too. They exchanged a silent look of understanding before Heather returned inside.

I made a good call letting her join the crew.

Once she was gone, I turned my attention back to Georgia who seemed even more conflicted.

"How do I know you'll keep your word and not turn me in at the nearest Galactic station?" she asked.

A small, petty part of me that was upset about what she did to Lini and Inil. I wanted to throw her earlier words back in her face and tell her she'd just have to trust me, but that wasn't going to get us anywhere.

"What do I need to do so you'll trust me?" I returned the question.

Georgia stared back at me, her expressive eyebrows knitted together. "I'll never trust you."

I didn't know why that statement stung but it did, not that I could blame her if she'd been abducted by the Ska'av. Compared to them, Georgia was barely a pirate. She wasn't even a bad person, just a damaged individual that could do with some kindness and compassion.

And that started with me.

I reached for the key in my pocket. "Hold out your hands."

She did as I asked, remaining silent as I undid the cuffs and put them away. This was a big gamble, but it wasn't like I had another choice. Whether I liked it or not, Georgia was the one making the decisions here. If she didn't like my offer, I'd have to hand over my cargo if I wanted to get out of here.

Georgia stared at me, her eyes darkened. "What if I decline?"

"Then I'll hand over as much cargo as your ship can carry and you can go back to this... life, if that's what you want to call it. Robbing good people, travelling from abandoned planet to abandoned planet without anywhere to belong. Never returning to Earth and finding your family," I said. To show her I meant it, I opened Aba's cage.

The bird flew out instantly and collided with Georgia. She squealed and tried to perch him on her arm, something he didn't seem very good at. His claws dug into her arms, leaving red streaks, but she didn't seem to notice. Instead, she babbled sweet nothings in a high voice and Aba repeated them eagerly. Her face lit up with a real smile and it was wonderful to see her eyes sparkle. Watching them together, it was clear there was a soft side to the stoic Georgia, and I was eager to see more of it.

She turned to me, her face back to a neutral expression, but it didn't hold nearly the same mystery anymore. "What about my ship?"

"We can leave it here or take it with us. We have enough space in the cargo hold."

"And you won't turn me in to the authorities?"

"No, you have my word."

"Your word means nothing to me."

I chuckled at her retort; that was exactly what I thought she'd say. "It doesn't have to mean anything to you. You just have to know how much my word means to me and that I'll honour it. It's your choice. If you give me the anti-virus, I will take you to your planet. If you don't, you can have my cargo and we'll never see each other again."

The way she looked at me with her piercing eyes made it feel like she was staring right into my soul. I wondered if all humans liked eye contact so much or if it was just her.

"I get to take my ship and Aba?"

"Yes, you'll be a guest on my ship."

"I'll need to access my ship to get the anti-virus. Alone," she said.

I gestured to the cage. "You can, but Aba will stay with me."

Georgia raised one eyebrow. "You don't trust me?"

"No, I'd be a fool to trust you."

"Then why should I trust you?"

"Because I'm the person who responded to your call for aid. I haven't harmed you or your bird."

She pressed her forehead against that of the bird. Some strange way of communicating? Maybe I'd done it all wrong, relying on the animal's random exclamations. With a deep sigh, Georgia wrangled Aba back into the cage that I was holding open. The bird stared at me with four angry eyes, clearly not happy to be separated from its owner again already.

"You won't have to wait for her for very long," I told it soothingly.

A tickle at the tip of my ears made me look at Georgia. She was watching me strangely.

"You're talking to my bird." It was a statement, not a question.

"Yes, we've had some interesting discussions already. Isn't that right, Aba?"

I didn't really expect the bird to respond, but to my surprise, he cawed, not looking as angry anymore. "Georgia! Ella! Bee! Georgia! Aba!"

"He knows my name," I cooed before I could stop myself. Aba pushed his chest out in pride. Or maybe I was just seeing what I wanted to see.

"He doesn't usually talk to other people," Georgia

muttered. "I hope you didn't teach him any naughty words. He knows way too many of them already."

"You swashbuckling waste of galactic space!" Aba responded gleefully, as if to prove a point. "Rak, rak, rak!"

I ignored the bird and pointed at the pirate's little cruiser. "If you want this deal, you better go and set up the anti-virus."

[13]

GEORGIA

I felt her piercing stare on my back all the way to the entrance of my ship. My steps were heavy with doubt. Was I really going to just hand over the anti-virus to the captain? I couldn't trust her. I couldn't trust anyone. I'd never met an alien who stuck to their word. Ellabee wasn't the first one who'd tried to charm me with pretty promises. In the end, they'd turn out to be empty. She was going to betray me, just like everyone I'd met since my abduction. Aba was the only reliable being and he was, well, a parrot. Not exactly a role model.

Everybody lies. It was my mantra. The first rule of my pirate handbook. They lied, so I lied in return. Honesty got you killed. And I didn't intend to die any time soon.

But there had been another human, Heather. Was

she lying as well? Was she in on Ellabee's deception? Or...

I didn't dare to hope. Hope was just as deadly as honesty. I was so close to my goal. Only a few more ships to free of their cargo and I'd have enough credits to get home. I had to lie low after every robbery, so it would take me at least a year, maybe longer. And every time I ran the risk of my prey killing me out of anger for getting them caught in my trap. I had enough scars to prove that being a pirate was a dangerous business.

Maybe I should risk it. Maybe I could trust Ellabee and Heather. Passage home... it seemed too good to be true, but didn't everyone deserve some luck at least once in their life? I'd been through so much shit that I was owed some luck.

The inside of the ship was utter chaos. Ellabee or her crew had clearly searched every inch of it in the hope of finding the anti-virus. My belongings were strewn across the floor, drawers stood open, and several alarm lights were blinking frantically. I gritted my teeth. They could have at least cleaned up after themselves. Not that I was surprised in the slightest that they'd searched the ship. Everyone did. It's why I didn't keep any truly personal things on board. Not that I had many of them.

I sat on my chair and winced at the angle the back was now set to. Someone much taller must have been sitting here while I'd been in captivity. I hated other people using my stuff, especially my super-comfy pilot chair. I readjusted it until I was comfortable again, then turned off the security alarms one by one. Out of curiosity, I opened some of the computer logs to see what Ellabee's technicians had done to my ship. It was the usual; some scans, some attempted hacks, some physical attacks on the interfaces. Nothing new there. If I ended up accepting Ellabee's offer, I could bargain for something by training her crew to be better at this. It was always good to keep several aces in my hand, just in case.

Now that the lights had stopped blinking, I could focus on the next step. Option one was to take off, escape to freedom, leaving Aba behind. No way. He'd saved my life more than once. I wouldn't abandon him now.

Option two was to take Ellabee's offer. Give her the anti-virus in return for passage to Earth. I didn't even need her cargo if she got me home to my planet. Alien products would be more trouble than worth there. It would be hard enough to explain my absence. I wasn't quite sure how much time had passed there, as none of the alien calendars matched that of Earth, but it had to be at least ten years. I didn't even know if my dad was still alive. Was he still searching for me or had he given up hope long ago? And would he believe my crazy story? I'd imagined so many times how our reunion would go. In my nightmares, my dad didn't believe me and pushed me away. In my dreams, he welcomed me back with open arms, giving me the happy life I craved.

Option three. Deceive Captain Ellabee yet again. Pretend to accept her offer, then steal her cargo and run as fast as I could. Or take over her ship. If it was capable of travelling to Earth, I could force them to fly there without having to trust in her word.

The third option sounded the most reliable. It was something Georgia the pirate would do. But for a short moment today, when Heather had hugged me, I'd felt human again. The kind, gentle, nice girl I'd once been. Maybe it was worth a try.

I started typing, programming the anti-virus to be transmitted to Ellabee's ship. And if this failed and she betrayed me, there was always an alternative.

It didn't take too long for the anti-virus to reach Ellabee's ship. It would perk their operator up right away. Once that was done, I turned the encryption back on so nobody else could commandeer it. Some people would call me paranoid, but I wasn't going to take any chances.

Once Ellabee had full control of her ship, that was when I was at my most vulnerable. If she was going to lash out, it would be now. Weirdly enough, I kind of hoped she would. It would be reassuring and familiar, whereas this whole thing was just bizarre. Why would she want to help me when all I did was trick, threaten, and mock her?

I got up from the pilot chair and gathered things from around my ship that I didn't want to lose. I didn't know if I'd be able to keep them on my person so I figured I'd hide them in one of my usual spots and return for it, if Ellabee turned on me.

With a last look at my thrashed lounge, I heaved my

backpack over my shoulder and got out from the side exit where nobody else could see me. There was a nearby hollow tree that I'd used before to keep some supplies, so I stuffed my belongings in it. There was a good chance I wouldn't be able to come back to retrieve them, but at least they couldn't be used against me.

Even though my ship was coming with me, I gave it a little pat on my way back, just in case this was all going pear-shaped. "Thanks, B3RR-Y. You've been a good home."

Without the virus, I had a lot less power and control over the situation and that was terribly scary. Still, I also felt something I didn't even know I was capable of anymore.

Hope.

[14]

ELLABEE

I pressed my wrist against the scanner and the door to the cabin slid open with a hiss. It was a little dusty since nobody had lived here for a while, but it would do well for my new... guest.

"How's this?" I asked, gesturing around.

Georgia observed the room with those sharp eyes of hers, swiping a finger over the shelf and letting out a little hum. She didn't say anything and paused by the sleeping pod, examining it carefully.

"I updated it so it has a sleep setting," I said quickly. "It's what Heather uses."

"You expect me to sleep in a coffin?"

"Coffin?" I echoed, not sure if I misunderstood the word or if it was translated badly.

"Yes, a coffin. For dead bodies," she said as if that explained anything.

"You keep dead bodies in a sleeping pod?"

"We put dead bodies in a coffin and then put those in the ground. We sleep in beds. They're flat." She patted the top of the pod. "Not a claustrophobic nightmare."

I wasn't sure what exactly the issue was here, I hadn't heard Heather complain, but I also didn't know what her and Atina's sleeping arrangements were like. That was none of my business, even if I had to admit to being curious about the compatibility of humans and Kyvens.

"Do I need to find you something else?" I asked.

She shook her head and carefully placed Aba's cage on a low table. "Nope, I'll be fine in the coffin. In some ways, it's like I'm dead anyway."

"Okay...?" I frowned. "Can we circle back to putting dead people in the ground? What's that about?"

"It's a whole thing; humans are clingy, they have trouble letting go," she replied flippantly. "Anyway, so this is my cabin now, huh?"

I nodded. "Yes, I'll set it so it's controlled by your implant. Only you'll be able to enter and exit."

She gave me a sceptical look. "And I can leave and go as I please?"

"You can go anywhere you want, except the bridge. I'm not having you anywhere near the command centre in case you try to hijack my ship again," I half-joked. As much as I wished I could trust Georgia, she'd already proven that she was wily and not above resorting to dirty tactics.

To my surprise, she gave me half a grin. "That's fair. So how long until we'll reach Earth?"

"I'm having my operators calculate the route now, but they're slow booting up because they've just recovered from a bad virus," I quipped.

Georgia's shoulders dropped and she scratched the back of her neck. "Sorry?"

"You can apologise to them if you mean it."

"I might. Have they fully recovered?" She actually sounded concerned.

I nodded. "We'll be able to take off before sunset, I think. I need to talk to the pilots to get ready for take-off."

"Ready for take-off," Aba echoed. The bird had been snoozing, but now its four eyes were wide open.

"He will have to get used to his new home," Georgia said thoughtfully. Somehow, I was sure she wasn't just talking about her pet. "Will your crew have an issue if I let him fly around freely? Will they know he's not food?"

I wasn't sure if she meant it as an insult, but it sure felt like one. "My crew know how to behave. They're not savages."

"Don't eat me, please don't eat me!" Aba screeched, his wings fluttering wildly. My implant translated his words before I could detect the language he'd spoken.

"It's alright," Georgia cooed, stroking his scaled cheek through the cage bars. She looked at him with such adoration, turning her permanent scowl into something soft. I couldn't help but stare. The human was gorgeous when she didn't look like she was about to skewer me. But as soon as she turned away from the bird, the magic dissipated as her mask slid back in place. "I think his species is raised for food. He didn't know a lot of words when I first got him, but what he said made me think that his previous owners didn't keep him as a pet."

I observed the animal with new eyes. He didn't look like something I'd want to eat, and not just because there wasn't much meat on his lean body. No, he seemed way too sentient to be farmed. Not that sentience stopped some beings from keeping others for food. Travelling through space meant I'd seen some truly wonderful things, but also some that I'd rather forget.

I couldn't help but shudder at the memory of the butcher halls on Kqwnt-2 where I'd once had to bring a load of cargo.

Shaking off the bad thoughts, I focused on the present. "I have a moment to show you around if you want. Unless you prefer to rest?"

She smirked wryly. "I rested for long enough in your cargo bay. So yes, give me the tour. I've not been on a ship this size in quite a while. Aba, want to come?"

"Georgia and Aba! Aba and Georgia!" The bird stretched its legs, showing off its sharp talons. As soon as Georgia opened the cage door, he flew onto her shoulder, playfully nipping the rounded top of her ear. For a moment, I had the overwhelming urge to touch her ear as well, to know what it felt like. But that was silly. Only mates tickled each others' ears. It was an intimate gesture reserved for intimate moments, so I really shouldn't feel that urge just now.

I forced myself to turn away and hurried out of the room. Maybe I needed a break. The last few days had been taxing. Us Kyvens didn't need to sleep like other species, but we did need to recharge occasionally. Once we were en route to Earth, I might take a well-earned break. I hadn't caught up with my favourite Kyven vid-drams in ages.

"Can we start with the bathroom or whatever you call the place you wash? I've not had a shower in ages." Georgia was following me, but I hadn't quite regained my control enough to turn and look at her.

"Of course. There is a hidden water bowl in your cabin that you can use both to drink and to wash your hands and ears, but we have larger cleansing stations down this corridor."

I led her to the closest bathroom and let her look around. She seemed familiar with the technology and didn't ask any questions.

"I'll take a shower when you have to get back to the bridge," Georgia announced happily. "Shall we get some food?"

She was taking control of my tour. Instead of finding it annoying as I would have with some members of my crew, I actually found myself smiling with amusement. She wasn't part of my crew yet, so she didn't have to treat me as her captain. It was refreshing. We were almost equals now that she was no longer my captive. I was still the only person in charge of the ship, but when it came to other things, there was no more hierarchy between us. When did I last have an equal to talk to? I'd become a captain at a younger age than most. Ever since, there had been an unspoken barrier between me and everyone else on board.

"Food!" Aba cawed. He really shouldn't be hungry. I'd given him all the Avillian nuts we'd had on board. Luckily, they weren't super expensive, but Katak wasn't too pleased about the depleted stash.

"Yes, we'll have some food," Georgia said in that loving tone of hers. She looked at me, frowning. "I hope the food is better than what you were bringing me in the cell."

I chuckled lightly. "It won't be, your food came straight from the canteen."

"That's a shame. I regret my decision to come aboard already," she said, turning away but not fast enough to hide the faint smile curling her lips up.

A warm sense of pride welled up in me that I'd managed to make her smile. I didn't know why it mattered to me, but I liked the idea of melting Georgia's icy exterior and finding out more about the person she was underneath all her snark and sass.

[15]

GEORGIA

There was something surreal about hanging out in a lounge large enough for Aba to fly around. Everything about Ellabee's ship was amazing. There was a large ceiling window that allowed me to watch the stars soar by and all other nifty bits of technology that were far more advanced than what I had.

It almost made me forget why I was here and what was at stake. Part of me still thought this was all an elaborate ruse and Ellabee was going to go back on her promise, but after flying for weeks, we could've easily reached a Galactic patrol station, and yet we hadn't. Did that mean she was actually taking me to Earth? Home?

I stared out the window at the stars flying past, trying to identify the constellations or clusters. I prided myself on being good at navigating without the need for technology, but we were in unknown territory now.

"Time for naps! Time for naps!" Aba croaked in my ear, nuzzling his beak into my hair.

I patted his head. "It's not sleep time yet."

"Time for naps!" he repeated stubbornly.

Silly bird. He'd been my constant companion for years. I didn't know what I'd do without him. Nobody was better at cheering me up when I was down and making me feel less crazy when I talked to myself. He was the best bird I'd ever known and that was a tough spot to get considering all the birds my grandfather used to own. So what would I do with him when we reached Earth...?

I'd never had any reason to worry about that, but as we were rapidly hurtling through space towards my home planet, it was something that I couldn't ignore much longer.

"Ellabee! Ellabee!" Aba cried, flapping his wings happily as he flew towards hers. He landed on her shoulder and I felt a pang of jealousy. It had taken me years to teach him that and he missed more often than not, but not when it came to her.

She gave him a little tickle under his chin, and he puffed the scales on his chest. *Show off.*

Ellabee gently removed him from her shoulder and put him down next to me, much to his dismay. He let out a protesting shriek and the tips of his wings flashed green.

"So, how're you finding the PoTA-2?"

I only had compliments for her ship, but I shrugged instead. "Ehhhh."

Her eyes widened and she put her hands on her hips in a way that showed off the muscles in her arms. "Ehh? This ship is so much better than your piece of crap. How does that thing even fly? It's basically glue and parts. You're lucky you haven't crashed."

"Who says I haven't?" I challenged.

"Have you?" There was genuine curiosity in her voice.

"Maybe. You?"

She leaned back against the hard material of the bench and stared up at space. "Once, when I was much younger and more reckless."

Despite pretending not to care, I felt intrigued. "What happened?"

"I don't want to go into the details, but there was a bad crash. I lost my ship, some of my crew, and learned a harsh lesson." She lifted her shirt slightly, exposing her hard abdomen and a long dark scar on her blue skin. "Got a memento in case I ever forget as well."

I caught myself staring and quickly drew my gaze up, making the mistake of looking into her eyes. I tried to avoid looking at aliens; it gave them too much power over me, but there was something different about Ellabee. She was so strong and yet, there was an underlying vulnerability to her that was just so human.

To distract myself, I tickled Aba's head. "You know, I've never said thank you for taking good care of him during the whole... thing."

She gave me an amused look. "He's fun. I like him. I've never known a bird to have so much personality."

"No, me neither. He's... family." It felt dangerous to admit how much he meant to me, but it was plain and obvious to anyone with eyes. Ellabee's were bright and sharp, with really beautiful irises. There was no way she didn't know how important he was to me.

Aba cawed softly and pressed himself into me. "Time for naps! Time for naps!"

A low chuckle came from Ellabee. "He said that a lot, but I don't know what a naps is. Maybe you could finally clear up the mystery."

"The word is actually 'nap'," I corrected her. "It's like a small sleep in the middle of the day."

"And it's different from your other sleeps?"

"Yes, it's shorter and there's nothing quite like it. But you don't sleep, right?"

Ellabee kicked her legs up. "Nope, and I don't know how you willingly put yourself in a state of unconsciousness like that. Isn't that scary?"

"Not more than being awake," I replied with a shrug.

"What's it like to dream?" Ellabee asked.

"What's up with you? Why are you so curious today?"

"I'm reading up on humans and Earth. There's a lot of demand for exotic products. The more I know about your planet, the better it'll be for securing the right things for my clients," she answered easily.

Somehow, I felt disappointed that her curiosity

wasn't about me, but I pushed that feeling away. I couldn't let my guard down, no matter how disarmingly charming she was. I had to remember who she was and what I'd done to her. People didn't just forgive so easily.

"How long until we reach Earth?" I asked, trying to shift the tone of the conversation.

"Not too long, a few centi-clicks."

"Oh, that's good. What navigation system do you use? Galactic Grid? Star System?" I asked, trying to be casual.

"Galactic Grid. Why? Are you trying to work out if you can use the ship if you hijack it?" There was a teasing tone in her voice, like she didn't actually think I would.

When did she decide I wasn't a threat?

"I just like to know where I am. It makes me feel safer." The explanation slipped out before I could stop myself. Maybe it wasn't just Ellabee who no longer saw me as a threat. The same seemed to be happening the other way round, too. I didn't want to trust her; I didn't want to trust anyone. It wasn't a good idea to rely on others. It usually ended in pain and disappointment. But it was hard to keep up the walls I'd built around myself. For the first time in ten years, I wasn't running from something. Instead, I was travelling home, surrounded by friendly people who didn't even once try to torture me. Life was strangely good. I'd almost be sorry to leave the PoTA-2. Almost. My father was waiting for me. My friends, if any of them even remembered me.

Last night, I'd thought about what coming home would look like. Until now, it had been an abstract goal that seemed unattainable most of the time, but now that we were getting closer to Earth with every day, I was beginning to be brave enough to picture my return in more detail. I'd been abducted before I'd even sat my GCSEs, so I'd have to return to school. I'd always planned to go to university and become a paramedic, but now I wasn't so sure of what I wanted. As much as I'd hated my life as a space pirate, there had been moments where I'd been almost happy. Mostly when I'd been messing with technology, fixing things, flying the ship. The thought of never being able to steer a spaceship again filled me with dread. Earth seemed strangely small after seeing dozens, if not hundreds of planets. What was I going to do there? Become an engineer? I didn't feel like years of studying. I wanted to earn my own living from the start, but all the jobs I thought of required at least some kind of training.

The one thing I didn't want to do was live with my father and be reliant on him. I wasn't the teenager who'd been abducted. I was an independent woman now.

"You've gone quiet. What are you thinking?" Ellabee asked gently. The way she smiled at me broke my heart. Soon, I'd have to say goodbye to her and never see that smile again.

"Home," was all I said.

Her smile wavered a little, but she quickly caught

herself. "I've been meaning to give you this. I know technology on your planet is still very basic, so... here."

She handed me a silver ring with a massive black stone embedded on the top.

I took the ring with apprehension. "What is this? Are you proposing to me?"

"Proposing what?"

"Nothing. Sorry. It's a human custom; I should have known it was something else. So why are you giving me a ring?"

"It's an interstellar communicator. I thought it would be better to disguise it as something that can be found on your planet. It's primed to your biosignals, so only you can use it. Just hold the stone against your earlobe and the holo interface will appear. Just in case you want to contact me - I mean anyone who isn't on Earth."

"Why my ear?"

Ellabee looked a little sheepish. "First thing that came to my mind. Anyway, it looks like I will be travelling to Earth fairly regularly from now on. There are some Kyvens that have human mates and regularly want passage or goods. If I'm in your area, I could message you. If you want, of course. Do you?"

"Yes," I blurted, surprising both Ellabee and myself.

"Phone home," Aba cackled, before launching himself into the air, circling the lounge. I watched him with a grin as he did some daring manoeuvres only a feather's width from the ceiling. Such a show-off.

It was a long time since I'd seen him this reckless,

and maybe the first time I wasn't worried. There were no predators here, nobody that would hurt him or me. I didn't have to think about where my next meal was coming from or about my ship breaking down or having nobody to talk to.

I glanced to my left where Ellabee was watching me with that smirk of hers, and I felt a strange rush of gratitude. Even if things could change at a moment's notice, right now, everything was perfect.

It was strange to admit, but for some reason, I wanted this moment to last forever.

[16]

ELLABEE

The day had come far too soon. We were about to enter the solar system that Earth was part of. Only a few more planets to pass, then I'd have to say goodbye to Georgia. Strangely, she'd grown from an enemy into something almost like a friend. I doubted she'd want to call what we had a friendship, but I was certain that's what it was. I missed her before she'd even left the PoTA-2. That surely meant we were friends?

I'd almost been tempted to ask Atina to slow the ship so that we had a few more days, but my sense of responsibility stopped me. Luckily. We had already lost so much time by being stranded on that miserable rock. Even though I wanted to be angry at Georgia for that, I couldn't. As much as she never spoke of what had happened to her, her silence told me more than she knew. I'd done some research into the Ska'av and every single thing I'd read about them was terrifying. They were monsters that hurt others for fun. It was a miracle Georgia had somehow survived with both her body and mind intact.

"Captain Ellabee?" Heather hurried towards me. Instead of being excited at returning to her home planet, the human appeared worried.

"What's wrong?" I asked more sharply than I'd intended.

She visibly looked around the room and I instantly knew what she meant. Even though everyone else on the bridge kept their focus on their workstations, I knew that they were all listening intently.

"Let's talk in my quarters," I suggested, noting her relief. I'd been right.

As soon as my cabin's door closed behind us, Heather activated her controlband. A picture of a human male appeared on the holo screen between us.

"I did some more digging into Georgia's family," Heather said breathlessly. "And I don't know how I didn't find this before, but-"

"What?"

"Her father died two years ago. I knew her mother died when she was five, so that means both her parents are gone. No grandparents that I can find. And she didn't have any siblings. That means..."

"She's alone," I muttered.

"Have you talked to her about what she plans to do when we arrive on Earth? Things are very different now than they were ten years ago. It's going to be hard for her to fit back in."

"No, we..."

I didn't tell her that I'd been reluctant to talk about the future with Georgia. I'd been all too happy to just stay in the present and enjoy every moment. We'd only agreed that Aba would stay with me, since he looked too alien to live with her on Earth. My ears itched with annoyance at myself. She wasn't prepared at all. I should have handled this in a much better way.

"Thank you, Heather. Can you send me the files?"

"Already done."

I was glad when Heather left. I sank onto my chair, letting go of all composure. I had to think. Had to find a way to tell Georgia that there was nobody waiting for her on Earth. No matter how tough she presented herself, that had to be devastating. At least if I got to break the news, I could sit her down, get her a drink—

The door to my quarters slid open with a buzz and I was about to chide whoever had come in without knocking until I realised it was Georgia, as if my thoughts had manifested her somehow.

I struggled to stand up, my knees weak with the news I had to deliver. "Georgia..."

"I saw it!" Her eyes shimmered in an unusual way and her voice held more emotion than I'd ever heard from her. "Earth! I saw it through the window. It's actually Earth!"

"Yes, we'll land when it's night," I said. "So there's something—"

Georgia bridged the gap and took my hands in hers, an unprecedented gesture that made my fingers tingle. She let out a little squeak. "I can't believe you took me here? You took me here? Why?"

"I told you I wouldn't, didn't I?" I replied weakly.

"Yes, but people never keep their promises. I'm so excited, I can't wait until we land. Can I give your pilots the coordinates so we land close to my hometown? I want to go see my dad first."

I stared at our joined hands, a painful lump in my throat. Did I really have to deliver the news? She was so happy and the childlike glee on her face was the most beautiful thing. I didn't want to be the one to dash it. Maybe I could just let her discover it for herself. She would know the truth soon enough. If I didn't say anything, she could have hope for a little longer.

Georgia did a little hop. "Thank you, thank you, thank you. I can't believe you took me here; you're the first honest person I've met in space."

Honest... The words echoed and restricted my three hearts in a painful way.

"Georgia... Before we land, I have to tell you something first." I gathered a breath, trying to find the right words. "I did some research on your abduction and your family and..."

"And?" she prompted, her smile so wide I could see her pearly teeth.

"Your father, he's... astralised."

"Astralised? What's that?"

I recalled the conversation we had earlier. "He's in a coffin in the ground."

Her smile faltered. "What? Why would you say that?"

"I'm sorry. I can show you the files Heather found, they have the record—"

Georgia pulled her hands out of mine and took a step back, the smile replaced by the same hostile look as when we first met. "I knew this was too good to be true. I don't know what you're trying to achieve, but I'm not falling for your trick."

"It's not a trick."

"I don't believe you. My dad isn't dead, you're making it up to hurt me."

"Georgia..."

"Don't you dare say my name like that," she sneered, her eyes hard and cold. "You're just saying this to keep me away from Earth, but I'm not going to fall for it. You will take me to Earth, to my hometown, or I will remote detonate my ship and sink yours in the process."

Her words were like a slap in the face, but I felt more hurt than angry. I should've known she was never going to trust me and that she'd have a backup plan in case we didn't do what she wanted. I didn't think she'd resort to mutual destruction, but I shouldn't be surprised.

I swallowed hard. "There's no need to resort to threats. I said I would take you to Earth and I will. But you're on your own after that."

"Good, I don't need you or anyone else. I can take

care of myself, I always have!" She stormed out, growled at the sliding door because it didn't slam, and stomped away.

I was a fool for thinking Georgia and I could ever be friends or equals.

A part of me wanted to chase after her, but what good would that do? It was obvious that she didn't trust me. Soon, she would be out of my life. I didn't know why that bothered me so much, but it didn't matter. She couldn't have been clearer about how she saw me.

[17]

GEORGIA

The tense silence in the pod was overwhelmingly loud. I didn't know why Ellabee insisted on coming all the way down to Earth with me. Maybe it was part of her master plan to make me pay for what I did to her operator. I didn't know why she would bother with an elaborate ruse like this, but what she said about my dad had to be a lie.

It had to be.

Because if it wasn't....

A small shock travelled through the pod as it made contact with the ground, catapulting me into Ellabee. Her strong hands steadied me and for a moment, I forgot all about her lies and betrayal. It was just so nice to have someone look out for me.

"You okay?" she asked, her concern so believable I almost fell for it.

"Yeah, fine." I shrugged her away and fought the urge to hug myself. I wouldn't have to put up with these aliens for very long. Within a few hours, I would be back home and then all of this could be just like a bad dream. If only I could have taken Aba with me. He was back on the ship, now officially living in Ellabee's quarters. Despite our argument, she was the only person he trusted.

I undid my safety buckles and jumped up, away from Ellabee with her fake concern and fake sympathy. I should never have let my guard down. I should have known better.

The moment the doors slid open, I ran out of the pod. A blast of fresh air hit my face. Earth air. I breathed it in deep. For a second, I felt dizzy.

When I'd visualised my return home, I'd seen myself fall onto my knees and kiss the ground. I did no such thing in reality. I knew Ellabee and the others were watching me. I didn't want to appear weak.

I blinked a few times and the dizziness passed. We'd landed in an abandoned parking lot on the outskirts of town. I knew this place, had been here as a kid. If things hadn't changed from back then, nobody would come here until nightfall, when the local teenagers arrived with six-packs of beer and the occasional joint. I'd only been a few times before aliens had stolen my youth. I'd never been drunk on Earth alcohol. Why did that make me sad? There were worse things.

"This is...nice."

I had to hide a grin at Ellabee's attempt to compliment the car park. I wasn't sure if she'd ever stepped foot on Earth before. I kind of hoped this wasn't her first impression of my planet.

"Thanks for the ride. I guess you can keep my ship. Don't worry, it's not actually going to explode. I was bluffing."

I turned away from her before my emotions betrayed me. Despite everything, I had enjoyed my time on the PoTA-2.

"Goodbye," I muttered while walking away. My legs felt heavy. Gravity was stronger here than on the last few planets I'd visited. Or maybe it was because my last memory of walking on Earth was as a teenager. I'd grown since then, in body and mind.

"Wait!" Ellabee shouted from behind me. "I'll come with you."

"No. Don't."

I didn't turn to look at her. Just walked away. And she didn't follow.

The streets looked both familiar and strange. Most shops I remembered were gone, replaced by new ones. A few houses had been pulled down completely, leaving ugly gaps in the roads of my memory. In the distance, tall towers had been raised in my absence. They were ugly and didn't match the rest of the town.

I forced myself to search for the positive changes. New flowerbeds at the market square. A poster about a new youth centre. A few electric cars replacing the old-fashioned petrol guzzlers.

But it was hard to see the good when my memories were so much better, sparkling with happiness and joy, while this all looked bleak and disappointing. No. That was just a momentary illusion. As soon as I got home, everything would be back to normal. Just around this street... And there it was, my house. My dad and I had lived on the upper floor of a Victorian villa that had been converted into flats long before my birth. The house looked just like I remembered. The front garden was a little more tidy, with the first spring flowers starting to bloom.

An unfamiliar woman stood outside with a pram. New neighbours?

I slowly approached her, suddenly not sure of what I was supposed to do. Just knock on my dad's door? He was a decade older now. I didn't know what his health was like. I didn't want to give him a heart attack. Maybe I could ask that woman to prepare him for my arrival. We'd always had a good relationship with our neighbours. Auntie Clara downstairs had often babysat me as a child after my mum had passed away. Clearly, Clara had moved away. Hopefully. I didn't want to imagine the alternative.

"Hello," I called out to the woman. "Do you live here?"

She looked at me curiously but not unkindly. "I do. How can I help you?"

"Do you know Jack Stockwood from upstairs? Does he still live here?"

I knew it before she even opened her mouth. Saw it

in her eyes. And I realised I'd known from the moment Ellabee had told me.

Dad was gone.

The woman rocked her pram slightly. "No, we live upstairs. We bought the place after the previous tenant died. He left quite a mess. He was one of those hoarders who believed in alien abductions and collected all sorts of junk. It took my husband weeks to clean it all up. Why? Was Jack a friend of yours?"

I balled my hands, needing the sting of my nails to keep my composure. "Something like that. Do you know if he... No, you know what, never mind. Sorry for bothering you."

She gave me a friendly smile as she continued on her way, but I barely registered it. I just stared up at the windows of the flat that I used to call home. The curtains were different and if the woman was to be believed, everything inside too. Even though I was looking at it, it didn't feel real. This wasn't how I'd pictured it, how I imagined coming home. Even in my worst nightmares, where Dad had a new family and forgotten all about me, he was never not here.

Looking at the house was too painful and I set in motion. What was I supposed to do now? I'd dreamt of returning home for so long, it was what I imagined to endure the pain during my time with the Ska'av, what kept me sane in my lonely travels. What was the point of surviving when the thing I was living for was gone?

I fiddled with the new ring around my finger, twisting it while I considered my options. A small foolish part of me wanted to call Ellabee, but I doubted she'd reply after the way I'd acted. I'd lashed out like the teen that had been taken from Earth, not as the adult that I'd become, and I regretted the unceremonious way I'd left after everything she'd done for me.

I didn't know or care where my feet were taking me until I was standing in front of the diner across from my old school and realised I'd retraced the steps of my youth. To my surprise, it looked exactly the same, from the fake shrubberies in the planters to the old leather booths inside. Standing here, it felt like I'd been transported back in time but my reflection in the window grounded me in reality. Gone was the bubbly teenager with braids and a wide smile. Instead, a joyless lean woman with hollow cheeks and dark eyes stared back at me. Was that happy-go-lucky teenager still somewhere within me? Most days, I wasn't so sure of it, but I hoped she was.

My gaze latched onto the menu and I saw they still did milkshakes. I went in without thinking. It wasn't like I had anywhere else to go.

[18]

ELLABEE

Standing in front of the large window, my reflection was all wrong. The pigment-less colour of my skin made me look ill and my brown hair just looked wrong. While I admired the LightScreen technology, I couldn't say I loved the results. Unfortunately, this was what I had to put up with to avoid standing out.

I didn't know if Georgia had turned on the interstellar communicator on purpose or not, but I didn't want to take any chances and miss out on her call for help.

Despite my apprehension, I entered the shop and slid into the booth opposite her.

She looked up at me with a blank gaze. "What are you doing here?"

I pointed at the ring on her hand. "You sent me a signal."

"I didn't," she replied while twisting the ring around her finger. It was clearly an involuntary nervous tick.

"That turns it on," I said, trying to ignore the disappointment welling up in me. She hadn't wanted me here after all. It was just me that had grown irrationally attached.

Georgia slurped her drink through her straw, her expression neutral and impossible to read. "I was awful to you. Why did you come?"

That was a good question. Why did I?

"I don't know," I told her earnestly. "I'll go."

"Have you ever had a milkshake?" she asked before I could get up.

I took that to mean that she did want my company, so I remained seated. "No, I don't think so. I've been to Earth a few times, but I don't usually leave the ship."

She pushed her glass towards me. "Try it."

Part of me worried about having a bad reaction to the thick pink substance, but it had an appealing fragrance despite looking like poison. I took a sip, deciding it was worth the stomach ache if it was indigestible. The sweetness took me off guard and I savoured the fruitiness.

"That's really good," I said, licking my lips to get every last drop.

"Yeah, strawberry is my favourite because it reminds me of my childhood. I used to come here every Sunday with my dad. It became a ritual after my mother passed away. Guess that won't happen again..." The sadness in her voice told me she was no longer in denial about the truth.

"I'm sorry, Georgia."

She shrugged, but I saw through her. She was hurting.

"Is there anything I can do?" I asked. "Maybe you'd like some distraction?"

"Your looks are distracting enough. You look weird." There was almost a hint of a smile in her voice.

I played with the LightScreen ring. "It's the first time I've used this camouflage technology. I don't think I like how it makes me look."

"And you didn't have to turn your hair brown. Humans can have white hair."

I reached up to touch my head. "They can?"

"Yes, it's usually a sign of age, but it's okay."

"Oh, great. I'll change it back then," I said, reaching for my ring.

Georgia's hand flew on top of mine and she leaned in, her voice reduced to a low whisper. "Not in the middle of the diner."

I couldn't think of anything else than her warm hand on mine and how it made my stomach flutter in response. She noticed me staring and quickly pulled her hand back.

"How long are you going to stay here?" she asked after a while.

"A few of this planet's rotations. It depends on how fast I can procure all the cargo I need. I told Heather and Atina that they have four Earth days until I require them back on the PoTA-2. The two of them wanted to spend some time alone in a country named after one of your ocean creatures. It sounded like a very pretty place."

"Ocean creatures? Oh, Wales! It's not quite spelt the same way, we add an extra letter for the animal, but I suppose it doesn't matter. I've only been to Wales once, on a school trip, and... Sorry, I'm rambling."

Georgia clearly wasn't her usual stoic self. I could sense her suffering just beneath the surface. I wished she'd let me help her. I wanted to take her into my arms and hold her for as long as she needed, but I knew she'd push me away. She was a very stubborn female, one of the things I liked about her.

"It is okay to ramble. I will listen." I smiled at Georgia, trying to put all my sympathy for her into my gaze.

"No, I better shut up. Do you want another milkshake? You should try the chocolate one. In other places, they use really cheap cocoa powder but here they use proper dark chocolate to make them. They even have one with a flake. Do you want one?"

I nodded, mostly because it seemed she needed something to do. She gave me a tense smile and headed to the counter. I watched her as she joined a queue of other humans. Even though they were all similar with their non-blue skin, rounded ears and colourful hair, Georgia stood out from the crowd. She held herself differently. She projected the confidence of someone who had fought for her life and survived. She may be struggling now, but I knew she'd be alright in the end. And I'd help her through it. Whether she wanted me to or not.

"Here you go."

Georgia put a glass of brown liquid on the table before me. I hadn't even realised she'd returned. She'd got herself another pink hay-berry drink.

"Just in case you don't like the chocolate milkshake, then we can swap," she said when she noticed me looking at her glass.

That was so sweet of her. Thinking of my needs while mourning her father. I didn't know what to say to that.

Instead, I took a sip of the not very appetising brown drink. "Mmhm. That's really good. You have a good tongue."

"A good tongue?" Georgia echoed.

"Yes. Your tongue tastes well. Is that not how you say it in your language?"

She smiled, although no happiness touched her eyes. "No, we'd say that you have a good taste, not a good tongue. What you said might be misinterpreted as something physical."

"Oh. Sorry. You have a good taste then, not a good tongue. Not that I'm judging your tongue. I know they're very important when humans do their mouth-kisses."

Now I was the one who was babbling. And by the stars, what was I even saying?

"Ignore all that," I said quickly. "This drink seems to be affecting me. Does it contain alcohol?"

"Just a lot of sugar. I didn't know Kyvens could get sugar rush."

“Rush? I’m not rushing anywhere.”

“No, it’s not literal. It’s more like your body reacting to the hit of sugar, like a shock."

I reached for my controlband and ran a quick diagnostic. "My vitals are normal. I'm not going into shock."

This time, her eyes sparkled for a moment, just like they used to whenever she laughed. "Not that kind of shock. When children eat too much sugar, they get really hyperactive and loud. My mum never let me eat sweets after dinner because she said it would stop me from falling asleep. My dad did the opposite. He gave me a bedtime treat every night before he read me a story. It was our tradition, even when I became too old for stories. He-"

Her voice croaked with emotion.

"You don't have to talk about him if it's too hard. I'll be here to listen when you're ready."

"You will be?"

She seemed surprised by that. Did she think I'd abandon her on this planet despite her having nobody to stay with? She really didn't know me at all.

"If you want me to. You're always welcome on my ship. As a passenger or part of the crew. Or if you want to stay on Earth for a while, you can join us the next time we stop here. It's your choice. I remember how it felt when my parents were astralised. It's hard to think, hard to focus. But I'm here for you."

Georgia's eyes seemed strangely wet. She looked at me, her voice slightly shaky. "I need to think."

I nodded. That was to be expected and while I'd made the offer rather impulsively, it wasn't until I said it out loud that I realised that it was what I wanted. "Well, you know where we are and when we leave."

Georgia squeezed her eyes shut which somehow got rid of the water in her eyes. "I want to wander around a bit. Don't follow me, okay?"

"I won't," I promised.

It was hard to watch her walk away again, not knowing if she was ever going to come back, but at least we parted on good terms this time. If she wanted to stay on this planet and decided this was her home, I wished her nothing but the best. Even if it made all three of my hearts hurt.

[19]

GEORGIA

My hometown was nothing like I remembered it. After three days of bumbling around and living in a hotel room that I'd rented with a borrowed credit card, I had seen enough. It wasn't the new buildings or the changing technology that were jarring. It was the people. They looked at me differently, acted much colder and more indifferent. Nobody had time to talk, nobody wanted to help. I didn't really know how to get them to help. When I tried to initiate a conversation on the street or asked questions about my teenage self, they would scuttle away as soon as they could, clutching the hands of their belongings or children extra tightly.

I couldn't really blame them. My English was

broken, my accent harsh, my words cold. I gave commands and made demands. That was all I knew.

As humiliating as it was, standing in the middle of the busy square, the first tears in years streamed down my face. They were hot and burned and I couldn't stop sobbing no matter how much I wanted to. I cried like there was no tomorrow and not a single soul cared. If anything, people seemed to be walking around me to avoid me.

Standing here surrounded by humans, I'd never felt more alone and it properly dawned on me how much I'd lost, what the Ska'av had stolen. It wasn't just my childhood, my innocence; it was my ability to connect and relate and feel. They'd taken everything human about me and turned me into this cold, detached monster that didn't know how to help or be helped. The only person who cared about me was dead and I was more alone now than when I was a captor or a captive.

Someone touched my shoulder and I turned, expecting Ellabee even though I'd told her not to follow me. I'd tell her off after I let her comfort me.

My hopes were dashed when I looked at an elderly man with a hesitant smile and kind eyes behind thick glasses.

"Are you okay? Do you need a tissue?" he asked.

I sniffled and desperately tried to wipe the evidence of my sadness away. "No, I'm fine."

"Are you sure?" He dug a fabric handkerchief from his pocket. "Here, it's clean."

I almost pushed his hand away, but then I remembered how awful it felt to only ever rely on myself and I took the tissue. I even managed a grateful smile. "Thank you."

The stranger just smiled. "Do you want to talk about it?"

"Why would you listen?" I asked after blowing my nose.

"Because you look like you need it," he said simply.

After years of looking out for myself and surviving in space, I'd developed a pretty good gut instinct for spotting threats. He wasn't one.

"I just found out my dad is dead," I said, surprising myself. I was used to bottling everything up and locking away my feelings so they couldn't hurt me or be used against me. But no matter how hardened my muscles were from training or how rough my hands had become from surviving on my own, nothing could shield me from this pain.

The man nodded. "I'm sorry to hear that. I lost my mother when I was about your age, mind you, that's a long time ago now, but there are days when I remember it like it was yesterday. I don't know your situation, but if you want a word of advice from an old man, let yourself cry and grieve and you will heal."

Heal... Healing had never been on my list of priorities. I'd fought, protected, dreamt, hurt, but never healed.

"How do I heal?" I asked.

"Time heals," he said with a knowing smile. "Time, patience, and kindness."

For some reason, his description conjured an image of Ellabee in my mind. During our time together, she'd been nothing but patient and kind. Even when I was her captor and her captive. She'd treated me with respect, helped me without asking anything in return, and when we parted ways, she'd given me the one thing I hadn't had since the Ska'av had taken me. A choice.

It had overwhelmed me because I hadn't had the freedom to choose anything in so long. I thought I did when I was travelling on my own, but even then, I'd been trapped by my dream of returning home. But now that I'd been here and seen what it really was like, I was free.

I grasped the man by his hands, the first human hands I'd held in so long. "Thank you."

He chuckled lightly. "You're welcome?"

"My name is Georgia Stockwood. Please remember me when I'm gone," I told him.

"G-Gone?" he echoed, the worry clear in his voice.

"Not like that, don't worry. I have a ship to catch!"

I had never run this fast, at least not when I hadn't been running *from* something. Today, I was running *towards* something, my future. The tears dried on my cheeks as I hurried back to the abandoned car park where the PoTA-2 was parked. Ellabee would be waiting for me. I knew it. I slowed down a little when I realised I didn't know what to say to her. When we'd last talked at the diner, she'd offered that I could become part of her crew. Fly through space, but this time surrounded by friends, not all alone. It sounded like a dream. Or I could be a passenger, letting her take me somewhere far, far away. One of the nicer planets I'd visited on my travels. Maybe Ellabee could help me get a proper job, one that didn't involve stealing. Aba and I could settle down. But that would mean saying goodbye to the Kyven captain. A sharp pain in my chest made me stop. It wasn't just because I'd been running non-stop. The thought of leaving Ellabee for good physically hurt. It wasn't the same pain as the grief for my father and for the life I'd never got to live. It was a different sort of ache, a longing for a future yet to be written.

Others had determined my destiny for the past ten years. They'd ripped me from my home and forced me to do things I regretted. Now, I had a chance to change everything. A new beginning. It would no longer be just Aba and me against the universe. I had friends now. And I would fight for my future, even if it meant breaking the walls I'd built around my fractured heart.

[20]

ELLABEE

She was curled against my side, her eyes closed. I played with her hair, curling one lock around my fingers. She was so warm, so soft. I held the strand of hair to my nose and breathed in deeply. She smelled of home. Georgia sighed in her sleep, her lips opening just a fraction. I couldn't wait until she woke from her sleep and we could-

"Captain! Captain Ellabee!"

I woke from my recharge, the last flickers of the trance still running through my mind. My mouth was dry. I'd never had a trance this vivid before.

"Captain?"

Atina stood next to my pod, looking impatient.

I unplugged myself and got to my feet, straightening my uniform. "What's the matter?"

"Your human has returned. She's waiting outside.

She says she wants to show you something before she comes in."

I didn't miss her calling Georgia *my* human. To my surprise, I didn't take offence to it. In fact, I liked the sound of it. Especially after the trance I'd just had.

My uniform was wrinkled, but I didn't want to waste any time. I hurried to the closest airlock, ignoring Atina's amused grin. I supposed this was payback for how I'd teased her for falling for a human.

The planet's only sun was starting to set, painting the sky in shades of fiery orange. I liked Earth's sunsets, they were so much more colourful than those on Kyven.

A lone person was perched on the railing around the vehicle parking lot, staring into the distance. Her hair was illuminated in the same copper shades as the sky, making her appear even more beautiful. My hearts beat a little faster at the sight. She'd returned. My human, indeed.

I'd hoped that she would come back. I'd given her the space she needed, knowing that eventually, she would be drawn back to me. I just didn't think it would be this soon. She'd needed time to process her father's astralisation. As much as it hurt that I couldn't help her with it, I was glad that she seemed to cope well enough to return.

"It's a beautiful evening," I said softly, so as not to startle her.

"It really is." She turned around, her eyes reflecting

the fiery light. "This might be my last sunset on Earth. I wanted you to be here for it."

I didn't know what to say. She was honouring me by letting me partake in this special moment.

"May I join you?"

She tapped the rusty railing. "It's not the most comfortable seat, but go ahead."

I climbed onto the metal bars, almost expecting them to crumble beneath our combined weight. This place had seen better days, but in this moment, it was the most beautiful spot on the planet.

A vertical post forced me to sit close to Georgia, so close our thighs touched ever so slightly. I could feel her warmth through my uniform. There had been more space to the other side of her, but I must have instinctively chosen this side where I'd have an excuse to be closer.

"It's so strange, I've been trying so hard to come back here, and now I'm about to leave after just a few days," she whispered. Her voice carried more emotion than she usually showed. Again, I was glad that she was feeling safe enough to share her feelings with me. Maybe that scene from my recharging could become reality, one day.

"We can stay a little longer if you want to. We're almost done loading the cargo, but if you need more time, I will come up with a reason to stay."

She smiled at me, making all three of my hearts jump a little. "No need. I've said my goodbyes. Now it's time to start anew."

"Then you've thought about my proposal?"

"I have. I-"

A caw announced Aba half a click before he settled on Georgia's shoulder. The bird happily rubbed his beak against her cheek before turning to me. I expected him to ignore me or rant angrily at me as he had the last few days, but instead, he leaned towards me and offered me his beak as well. I carefully rubbed my cheek against it. I couldn't shake the sensation that this was a special moment.

"He really likes you," Georgia breathed. "I've missed him so much."

"Ready for take-off!" the bird cried in response.

She laughed. "No, not yet. Let's just enjoy the sunrise, Aba. After that, we'll fly."

"Fly to the stars! Georrrrrrgia and Aba!"

I chuckled at the bird. He was simply adorable.

"And Ellabee," Georgia added with a grin.

"Georrrrgia and Aba and Ellabeeeee!"

"Clever parrot. Has everyone been nice to him?"

"The crew love him," I reassured her. "He's even managed to persuade Katak to part with his personal supply of Avillian nuts. I didn't think that was possible. Aba has become part of the PoTAT-2."

"Do you think I can, too?" she asked quietly, suddenly sounding a little unsure. "Will they forgive me for what I did?"

"That's a good question. I think they will, eventually. But you might have to make reparations."

Georgia nodded thoughtfully. "That sounds like it

would take a while. You sure you want me on the ship for that long?"

"You can stay as long as you like," I replied honestly. It felt like a dangerous thing to admit, but Georgia had just taken a big step towards me by showing up. I needed to let her know she wasn't just welcome. She was wanted.

I put an arm around her shoulders before realising what I'd done. I expected her to push me away, but after freezing for a fraction of a click, she leaned against me. I could barely breathe. I didn't dare to speak. This was the closest we'd ever been and nerves settled in my stomach.

She let out a soft sigh that tickled my skin. "Ellabee..."

This was the first time she'd said my name and I loved the way it sounded with her accent. "Yes, Georgia?"

"Thank you for taking me to Earth."

"I gave you my word, didn't I?"

"But why? Why would you help a miserable, hostile, unreliable, awful person like me?"

It was a good question, but thinking back to our time together, the answer came easy. "That's not how I saw you. I mean, you were hostile, but not the other parts. I thought you were savvy, resourceful, strong."

She twisted in my arm but didn't move away. "You thought all of that?"

"And more. As I got to know more about you, I

admired your resilience and survival skills. *Beautiful*," I admitted under my breath.

"You think I'm beautiful?" Georgia asked, her voice slightly strangled.

I just nodded. "I also thought it was sweet how much you loved Aba—"

"Aba! Aba's the best!" he interrupted with a happy croak. That little bastard kept ruining our moments.

"Yes, Aba." I gave the bird a little tickle and tossed some nuts towards the ship for him to chase so he'd give us a moment alone. I turned back to Georgia, finding her staring at me with a strange look in her beautiful eyes. I took the fact that she hadn't run away as a good sign so I kept talking. "Don't get me wrong, you were a knot in my bowels, but I've enjoyed getting to know you and I'd like to continue doing that."

"I'd like that too," she replied, shuffling a little closer. "You're the first person I've met that's made me feel... like myself."

"What did you feel like before me then?"

"Angry, scared, sometimes I felt nothing at all. But with you, I feel alive. Seen. Valued." She ran her tongue over her bottom lip, drawing my gaze to her pink mouth. "I don't really understand how I feel, but I want to be close to you. I... Don't laugh at me, but I think I kind of want to kiss you."

My hearts skipped a beat. "A human mouth kiss?"

She let out a nervous chuckle that made her nose crinkle. "Yeah, but I've never... I don't know how..."

"I've never mouth kissed before either," I whispered,

leaning closer in the way I'd seen Atina and Heather do. I'd wondered before about what it felt like but even though it wasn't part of our culture, I always understood it was something intimate that wasn't any of my business. But now I could find out for myself and that was even more exciting.

Our lips met, softly at first. Georgia's mouth was warm and I could tell she was holding her breath. The friction of her lips against mine sent tingles down my body and I felt electrified in a way I had never felt before, not even from an ear tickle.

She pulled back just enough so she could look at me. She looked strangely vulnerable but not fragile like before. "That was nice."

I touched my lips, chasing the echo of the mouth kiss. "I like that a lot. Maybe we can do more of that when we're back up in space? If you're ready to leave."

Georgia nodded firmly. "I am. This town isn't home, not anymore. The place that I wanted to return to only exists in my memories."

"I'm sorry." I wrapped my arm back around her. "I know I can never replace what you've lost, but we can build something new. Together."

She leaned back in to kiss me, and I savoured the warmth flooding through me. Behind us, Aba let out a loud caw that made it clear he finished his nuts.

Georgia snickered into our kiss. "You're going to need a lot more Avilian groundnuts."

"We better get going then," I said, gesturing to the ship.

Georgia nodded and with intertwined hands, we made our way back up the ramp. Once we were at the top, we both turned to watch a little bit more of the sun setting on her planet. The day was over and somehow, it felt like the end of something else too. But tomorrow, a whole new life was waiting for us far beyond the horizon, and I couldn't wait to soar through the stars with Georgia by my side.

EPILOGUE

SEVEN MONTHS LATER

ELLABEE

Aba puffed up his scaled chest and trumpeted yet another awful noise that he thought was a song. As good as he was at mimicking voices, he sucked at singing.

"No, Aba, it's not Christmas yet!" Georgia laughed. "If you need to sing, choose something different."

She set a bowl of snacks on the low table in front of us, then snuggled back against me on the lounger. I'd got rid of my one-person podchair long ago, making space for furniture that would accommodate both of us.

"What's Christmas?" I asked over the noise of Aba's screeching.

"A human celebration that happens every December. Its roots lie in religion, but it's basically a time when family and friends get together, have big meals, sing songs, give each other presents, and go to church if they're religious. Wait, what month is it on Earth? It was spring when we left and that was quite a while ago. Let me check."

While she browsed her tablet, I popped some crackers into my mouth. They melted as soon as they hit my tongue, coating it in sticky sweetness. Yummy. We'd only just left Pluto-2, home of some of the best sweet factories in this sector of the galaxy, and were now headed back to Kyven to offload cargo and take on new supplies. With no other stops scheduled until we got to my home planet, I was looking forward to a lot of time with Georgia. The crew had learned to accept that when I was in my cabin with my mate, I wasn't to be disturbed unless it was for emergencies. Katak had stepped up a lot, as had Atina, although she was frequently distracted by her own mate, Heather. I was glad I'd never set any rules against working with your mate on board the PoTA-2. I would have sorely regretted those now.

"It's two months until Christmas," Georgia muttered, suddenly no longer cheerful.

"What's wrong?"

"The last time I celebrated was with my dad. We made a gingerbread house together, like we always did, but I was a silly teenager and kept complaining that it was childish. If I'd known that it was our last ever Christmas together..."

I pulled her closer and pressed a kiss onto her forehead. "I will celebrate with you if you want. We can even travel to Earth. I have a few clients who've requested items from there and I keep putting them off because we have other things to do. What do you think about that?"

Before she could reply, my controlband vibrated. Rak. Bad moment. I was about to dismiss the notification when I saw the name.

"This is an old friend calling me. I've not heard from her in ages. I wonder if there's something wrong. Do you mind if I take this?"

"Go ahead." Georgia pointed at the snacks. "Just be quick or there may be nothing left."

I started the holo call, making sure I was the only one visible.

"Khrista."

The curly-haired Kyven waved at me happily. She didn't look like she had bad news to share. "Hey. Have you ever been to Earth?"

I suppressed a laugh. If only she knew. I tapped my chin as if I was thinking hard. “Earth... That’s the non-Galactic Union planet with the five-fingered kyvenoids, isn’t it? I’ve been a few times on requests.”

Next to me, Georgia snorted with laughter.

“You think you could collect something for me? I don’t have a lot of credits to finance the trip, but I can get you tickets to the next Rotark20 Rally.”

Khrista knew me so well. Back when we'd been students together on Kyven, we'd gone to every single Rotark rally we could afford. I hadn't been to one in ages, but maybe it was time to introduce Georgia to my hobby.

"Really? I thought that was all sold out."

She grinned. "I know a Lilypian. What do you think?"

She'd already hooked me, but I pretended to hesitate. "I have a client who regularly needs things from Earth. I could see if he wants to place a request and pick up your goods at the same time. Which is what exactly?"

"A reindeer."

Georgia sucked in a sharp breath. She clearly knew what Khrista was talking about, even if I didn't have a clue.

"It's an animal," Khrista explained.

"Ah, I see. I'd need a special permit for transporting live goods from a non-GU planet. I've been meaning to get one, though..." I ran my hand through my hair. "How many Rotark20 tickets can you get your hands on?"

"Two?"

"I want four. And you're financing the special crew member I need for your... reindeer."

"I might be able to do three. And instead of financing, what if I came instead? You know I can handle myself on a ship and I have some knowledge of the planet, so I know what I'm looking for. I also might be able to secure you another order, I have some friends who regularly need things from Earth."

I didn't really need any more orders just now, but it might come in handy in the future.

"That deal is acceptable to me."

As soon as I ended the call, Georgia shimmied closer to me again. "Do you know what a reindeer is?"

"No idea."

"That's what I thought. You know how I told you about Christmas? Well, reindeer are associated with that. In some of the stories, they pull the sledge of Father Christmas."

"What do they look like?"

She showed me her tablet. A hideous animal with strange bony growths on its forehead looked at me.

"That looks weird. Why would you celebrate with such ugly animals?"

Georgia laughed. "They're not ugly, they're cute. I can't believe we're going to have a reindeer on board! It'll be like Christmas has come early. Do you think I'll get to stroke it?"

"You're my mate. You can do whatever you want on this ship."

She cupped my face and pulled me closer. "I love hearing you say that word."

"What word?"

"Two words," she whispered, her breath hot against my skin. "My mate."

Our lips were closing in on each other. Just before I finally kissed her, I said it again. "My mate."

I could taste her happiness in our kiss. I hoped, no, I *knew* it was the same for her.

Just to make sure she knew how important she was to me, I ran my finger over the rounded shell of her ear. She let out a sort of giggle, a sound that would've been unfathomable to imagine her making when we first met. She returned the gesture with loving care, her finger teasing the tip of my pointed ear. Sparks danced along my skin and I somehow fell even more in love with her.

Georgia's eyes shimmered as she nuzzled into me. "If we're picking up a reindeer, can we also get a tree? And lights? And gingerbread, mince pies, crackers, and—"

"We can pick up everything you want," I told her, fully serious. What was the point of having a cargo ship if I wasn't going to use it to make my mate happy?

She let out a sigh full of longing. "Thank you. It's going to be the first Christmas I celebrate since I was taken from Earth."

"I'm sorry you can't celebrate with your dad." I wrapped my arms tightly around her, hoping to convey how much I ached for her.

"It's okay. At least I get to spend it with family and that's really what Christmas is about."

"Family?" I croaked. That was a loaded word, not just for her, but for me as well. My crew was like family but it wasn't quite the same.

She nodded. "Yes, I mean Aba."

"Oh..."

Her laugh clattered through the cabin. "And you, you silly. You're so cute when you pout. I kind of like seeing the great Captain Ellabee pouty."

"You also like it when I'm stern," I remarked, raising an eyebrow and giving her my best withering stare.

"Yes, I do," she murmured, pulling me in for another kiss.

Life had never been sweeter. I had my own ship, an infinite amount of stars to travel through, and a beautiful mate that thought of me as family. I could never have predicted this outcome when I picked up her emergency signal way back, but now I was very happy that she'd tricked me into coming to planet Torrap. Neither of us was each other's captive anymore, but we were stuck together and I wouldn't have it any other way.

Thank you for reading The Alien's Falconer. We hope you enjoyed seeing Georgia and Ellabee's relationship develop as they gained more trust in each other. This book is part of ***Aliens and Animals****, a series of alien standalone romances with other characters you might recognise.*

Want to find out how pilot Atina met her human mate Heather? Read their story in ***The Alien's Shepherd****. Or start at the beginning with the first book in the Aliens and Animals series,* ***The Alien's Zookeeper****.*

If you're in the mood for more aliens and sci-fi romance, take a look at Skye's books: skyemackinnon.com/scifi

And if you want more f/f romance, check out Arizona's books: arizonatape.com

Don't want to miss a new release? Subscribe to our newsletters:
skyemackinnon.com/newsletter
arizonatape.com/subscribe

ALIENS AND ANIMALS

1. The Alien's Zookeeper - Bavalla and Tilly
2. The Alien's Veterinarian - Sahra and Abby
3. The Alien's Farmer - Tamsia and Rachel
4. The Alien's Shepherd - Heather and Atina
5. The Alien's Falconer - Ellabee and Georgia

skyemackinnon.com/aliensandanimals

ABOUT SKYE MACKINNON

Skye MacKinnon is a Scottish romance author who was raised by elves in the mystical Highlands and calls the Loch Ness monster her friend. Her bestselling books weave together romance with action, suspense and whimsical humour, creating page-turners filled with strong heroines, alpha heroes and loveable monsters.

Whether she's writing about aliens in kilts, hunky Vikings or cat shifter assassins, Skye likes to put a new spin on familiar tropes. Some of her heroines don't have to choose, some fall in love with other women, and others get abducted by clueless aliens.

Skye lives with her bossy cat on the west coast of Scotland and uses the dramatic views from her office as an inspiration, no matter whether she writes fantasy, paranormal or science fiction romance. Until she gets abducted by aliens, that is.

Subscribe to her newsletter:
skyemackinnon.com/newsletter

Join her Facebook Reader Group:
facebook.com/groups/skyesbookharem

ABOUT ARIZONA TAPE

Arizona Tape lives her dream life hanging out with her dog and writing stories all day. Her favourite books to write are urban fantasy and paranormal romances with queer leads, stories that she wished were around when she was younger.

When she's not writing, she can be found cooking up a storm in the kitchen, watching shows that make her cry, or trying her hand at her new hobby of the week.

She currently lives in the United Kingdom with her girlfriend and her adorable dog who is the star of her newsletter.

Sign up here for adorable pictures, free books, and news about her books: www.arizonatape.com/subscribe

FOLLOW ARIZONA TAPE

Website | Newsletter | Facebook | Facebook Group | Bookbub | Twitter | Instagram | TikTok

- https://www.arizonatape.com

- https://www.arizonatape.com/subscribe
- https://facebook.com/arizonatapeauthor
- https://facebook.com/groups/arizonatape
- https://www.bookbub.com/authors/arizona-tape
- https://twitter.com/arizonatape
- https://instagram.com/arizonatape
- https://www.tiktok.com/@arizonatape

Milton Keynes UK
Ingram Content Group UK Ltd.
UKHW010621080324
438959UK00001B/24